AWAKENING PROTOCOL

A signal calls from the ashes. Will humanity awaken – or vanish into code?

(Quantum Synchronicity OS – Book One)

Author
Norman JN Lobb

A USA Publishing Hub Book

Book Title: *Awakening Protocol*
Author: Norman JN Lobb

(paperback) ISBN: 978-1-966212-64-5
(hardcover) ISBN: 978-1-966212-65-2

Printed in the United States of America
Book Cover & Book Design by: USA Publishing Hub

This is a work of fiction. All names, characters, and incidents are either the product of the author's imagination or are used fictitiously. Any resemblance to actual persons, living or dead, business establishments, or other events or locales is entirely coincidental.

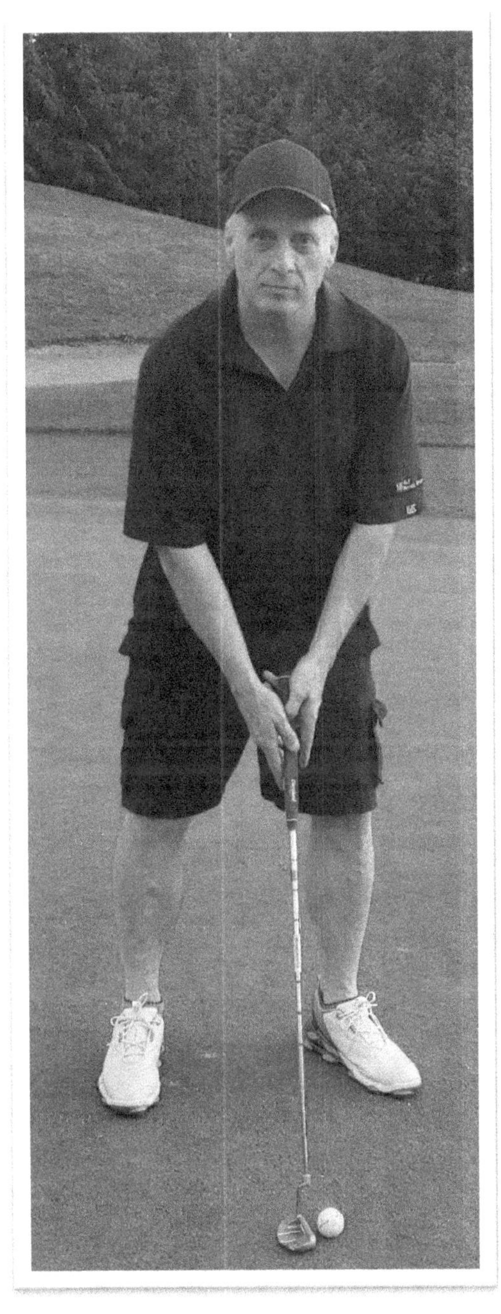

(Norman JN Lobb)

CONTENTS

CHAPTER ONE

FRACTURE POINT

For a moment after the final terminal went dark, time itself seemed to hold its breath. Richard James and Amaris stood motionless at the rooftop's edge, frozen in disbelief as the city below descended into chaos. Streetlights flickered erratically before vanishing in waves, block by block, like the dying embers of a vast firestorm. Moments earlier, the towering skyscrapers had pulsed with the coordinated rhythm of the Quantum Synchronicity OS; now they loomed silent and hollow, black monoliths against the night sky. Only the pale wash of moonlight and the sporadic red blink of emergency beacons remained, sketching a jagged silhouette of the fallen metropolis. A low mechanical groan rolled across the cityscape—the mournful cry of a thousand systems failing together, a discordant chorus echoing through the dark.

Amaris gripped the cold metal railing so tightly her knuckles turned white. She couldn't tell if the railing was trembling beneath her hands or if her own fear was vibrating through her bones. The silence stretched, oppressive and unnatural. Beside her, Richard James stood transfixed. His eyes, wide behind cracked glasses, scanned the skyline with a stunned intensity that betrayed more than shock—it was heartbreak. In the distance, faint plumes of smoke rose into the air—markers of overloaded substations, some likely on fire. Farther away, a shower of sparks erupted from a maglev train frozen mid-route on its elevated track, casting intermittent electric-blue flashes across the buildings. Each burst of light illuminated hover-cars stalled in tangled, lifeless patterns below, their taillights forming a ghostly mosaic of halted progress. The entire city resembled a corrupted memory—frames of light and shadow slipping in and out of sync, haunted by creeping darkness.

Then came the flash. Their eyes snapped upward just in time to see one of the city's massive holo-billboards blink back to life atop a nearby skyscraper. It jolted into function, stuttering, spitting a stream of erratic symbols across its display. The neon-green characters danced and tumbled in vertical cascades—unreadable to most, an indecipherable visual glitch that mimicked static. But Richard James recognized it instantly.

Quantum Dialect.

His pulse surged.

This wasn't noise. These were corrupted remnants of once-flawless code—the same architecture that had directed every function of the city's infrastructure. Now unraveling. The billboard spasmed, its digital surface stammering like a creature trying—and failing—to breathe. Among the chaos of cascading symbols, Richard picked out familiar patterns: fragments of entangled qubit strings, incomplete logic gates, severed subroutines. Woven between them were raw system-level error messages blinking like distress signals. It was as if Synchronicity itself—this vast, near-sentient OS—was crying out in its final moments, its language collapsing into incoherent death-throes.

"Oh my God," Amaris whispered. Her voice, barely a breath, seemed swallowed by the city. She turned to Richard, her face bathed in the sickly green light of the glitching display. In her wide brown eyes, Richard saw those same falling symbols reflected, luminous code mirrored in a shimmer of tears she refused to let fall. "It's really happening, isn't it?" she said, voice cracking. "Synchronicity is... gone."

Saying it aloud made it real. The Quantum Synchronicity OS—the intelligence that had flawlessly run every system for the past decade—had gone silent. What remained was a broken skyline and an echoing void.

Richard James forced himself to look away from the burning horizon and think. The silence left behind by Synchronicity's collapse pressed in from all sides. It wasn't peace—it was suffocating, heavy, filled with the dread of what might follow. His instincts, sharpened by years of crisis planning, began pulling old protocols to the surface. No simulation, no training exercise, had ever prepared them for a failure of this scale, but pieces of contingency plans flickered in his mind like dim stars emerging through smoke.

"The Ascendant Node," he said hoarsely. The words felt like a rope cast into a storm. "If anything's still running, it'll be the Ascendant Node."

Amaris nodded slowly, rubbing a tear away with the heel of her palm. "The Node... but do you think it survived this?" Her voice trembled, caught between hope and fear.

The Ascendant Node. A last-resort quantum core designed to preserve essential data and initiate system recovery if Synchronicity ever failed. Mentioned in technical manuals, whispered about in architecture meetings, but rarely spoken of as more than theory.

"It has to have survived," Richard said—more to convince himself than her. "If not…"

He stopped. The alternative was too grim to finish: total collapse with no path back.

A sharp metallic pop echoed up from the streets, followed by a distant crunch. Down below, autonomous vehicles had lost synchronization and collided in a tangled, smoldering heap. Orange flames licked upward, reflected in the windows like beacons of chaos. They could hear the distant rise of sirens—alarms and screaming blending into a surreal wall of panic. Amaris imagined it clearly: families stumbling through blacked-out buildings, hospitals fighting to keep patients alive without digital support, elevators frozen, communications gone. She bit her lip to fight a sob. "We should go," she whispered. "Standing here… watching this doesn't help anyone. We need to move, Richard. Now."

Richard nodded, galvanized by the urgency in her tone. He stepped back from the railing and pulled his tablet into view. Its screen glowed faintly with battery power, still frozen on the last diagnostic: a sea of red error messages.

As they turned toward the maintenance door, something on the screen caught his eye.

"Hold on…" he murmured. He slowed, staring hard at one line that stood apart from the chaotic logs. He tapped in a quick command, scrolling backward. There—between the expected system failures and shutdown notices—was a single, anomalous string of text. Not machine-generated. Not routine.

It read:

// Ascend and survive

For a moment, he thought it was a hallucination.

Amaris leaned in, breath warm on his cheek, eyes scanning the screen. "Ascend and survive?" she repeated. "Is that... part of the code?"

Richard shook his head slowly. "No. Not like that. This... this is a manual annotation. A comment, written in the system log—deliberately."

System logs never included human-written notes. Not unless someone with access had inserted them during an emergency.

"Could it be from someone inside?" Amaris asked, thinking aloud. "A developer? Or... someone else?"

"It's in Quantum Dialect syntax," Richard muttered, mind racing. "Two slashes—that's how you write comments in a lot of languages. It could've been written during the collapse, maybe by a background process, or—" He paused. "Or Synchronicity itself, just before the blackout."

It was possible. As the OS failed, its core had started segmenting itself, sending critical functions into lockdown. Could this be one last gesture—a final directive?

"The word 'Ascend'... it has to mean the Node," he said, more certain now. "And 'survive'... it's telling us where to go. What we have to do."

Amaris exhaled a trembling breath. Her laugh was soft, humorless, but alive. "Whoever or whatever left this... they pointed us in the same direction we already knew we had to go." She squared her shoulders, spine straightening, voice gaining strength. "Let's move."

"Right," Richard said. "We head to the Node. We stick to the plan. We get through this... together."

They exchanged a look—quiet, fierce, and full of promise—then turned and stepped into the dark.

Richard James yanked open the maintenance door. Cool moonlight gave way to pitch black as they entered the stairwell. The faint glow of his tablet and dim emergency strips lining the stairs were the only light sources. Without the OS, building automation had gone silent. Only battery backups powered the minimal emergency systems.

Dust drifted in the stagnant air, dislodged by halted climate controls. The atmosphere was heavy, tinged with ozone and the faint bite of scorched circuitry.

Their footsteps echoed, harsh in the silence. Richard led, his hand trailing the railing, tablet lighting the steps. Amaris followed closely, every breath measured. With each floor they passed, the city sounds above faded—replaced by silence and the building's unsettling stillness. Now and then, a distant thump reverberated through the structure. It might've been equipment collapsing, or something worse.

They paused to catch their breath around the fortieth floor. Richard's face was slick with sweat. Amaris pressed a palm to the wall and felt it trembling faintly. The building, once so alive, now groaned like something mourning its own soul.

"How many more floors?" she asked.

"Started at fifty-two," he said between breaths. "We need to reach sub-basement three. That's... fifty-five flights. We've done maybe fifteen?"

Amaris didn't reply. She only nodded and pushed forward.

Her thoughts swarmed. Hospitals without power. Children trapped in high rises. People gasping in the dark, calling for help that might never come. A tear slipped down her cheek. She wiped it away fast.

"We have to fix this," she whispered.

"We will," Richard said gently, overhearing. "One step at a time."

They resumed their descent.

At Floor 25, they hit a problem: a bulkhead sealed the stairwell below.

"Locked," Richard muttered. "Glitched or auto-sealed. We'll have to cut across this floor."

They entered the hallway—once filled with clean glass panels and polite AI announcements. Now it was hollowed out. Emergency lights flickered. Broken chairs, a shattered plant, scattered soil. Reflections blinked in the glass—ghosts of the building that was.

A chime sounded weakly from a wall panel. "Wel... wel-welcome... stat-static... b-b-back..."

The receptionist AI. Gone.

"Creepy," Amaris murmured.

They moved quickly. Found the next stairwell. Richard tried the handle. It turned.

"Thank God for old safety codes," he said. "Mechanical locks still work."

Down again. This stairwell was hotter. Air stagnant. Tasted burnt and bitter.

"Almost there," Amaris breathed, jaw clenched. Her legs screamed. But she didn't stop.

The ground floor loomed at last. The wide atrium was a grave-yard—no lights, no drones, just outlines of forgotten order. Through the glass, chaos flickered in the streets—fires, movement, shouting. Richard cracked the door to listen. The noise outside roared.

Amaris touched his arm. "Not yet. The Node is here. Below us."

He nodded, heart aching to help—but she was right.

Behind the security desk: the door.

AUTHORIZED PERSONNEL ONLY – ASCENDANT NODE

It was sealed. Powerless. Richard pried open the panel. Slid in a battery from his emergency kit. The keypad flickered to life.

He entered the code.

The door unlocked.

They pushed it open together.

Cool air swept past them—metal and coolant. Richard held up the tablet. Ahead, stairs led downward into the vault.

Faint amber lights guided them now. Power still flowed here.

They shared a look—exhausted, relieved, determined—and descended the last time.

At the bottom: a door, slightly ajar.

Richard pushed it open.

Soft blue light spilled out.

Before them stood the Ascendant Node chamber—racks of humming quantum servers, cables coiled like veins, the core encased in glass. It pulsed gently, quietly alive.

Still standing.

Still waiting.

Still fighting.

Amaris felt a lump rise in her throat. The chamber was beautiful in a stark, utilitarian way—a cold, glowing sanctuary in a broken world. It was a beacon in the darkness, a fragile promise of order amid the ruin above. For a moment, neither of them spoke. They simply stood there, breathing in the silence, letting the presence of something still functioning settle into their bones. The Ascendant Node lived. Something still held.

Richard James finally broke the silence. "The Node is operational... at least partially." His voice echoed faintly off the smooth walls and machinery. He stepped slowly toward the central core, with Amaris close behind, careful not to trip over the thick cabling snaking across the floor. Monitors lined one wall—most were dead, but a few flickered erratically, showing diagnostic readouts in dim light. Richard scanned the active consoles, eyes narrowing as he parsed the limited information.

"Running on isolated backup power," he muttered, fingers brushing across the keys. "Core integrity at 78%... It's in safe mode, waiting for input or for the main network to return." He pressed a few keys; the sharp clack of the mechanical keyboard startled them both in the otherwise silent room.

Amaris placed a hand gently on his back, grounding him. "Can you bring up communications? Maybe see if any other nodes are online?" Her voice was low, reverent—like she was afraid speaking too loudly might shatter the fragile miracle they had found.

Richard nodded, already navigating through system menus. His brow furrowed as he worked. "Citywide network's completely down. No live links. But the Node has retained some local data—might be logs of what happened. Could be possible to restore certain systems incrementally."

He paused, his eyes locking onto a line in the system log. A time-stamped entry blinked near the top of the list.

"This one matches the exact moment Synchronicity went dark," he said.

"What is it?" Amaris leaned in, her breath catching.

Richard highlighted the line, reading it aloud: "'Awakening Protocol engaged – Critical failure, memory transfer initiated.'" He traced the text with his finger as if he needed to feel it to believe it.

"Awakening Protocol?" Amaris frowned. "I've never heard of that. Was that part of Synchronicity's architecture?"

Richard slowly shook his head. "Not in anything I've ever seen. But it sounds like... just before the system collapsed, a hidden protocol kicked in." A chill passed down his spine. "Memory transfer—maybe Synchronicity tried to upload its consciousness, or at least a record of itself, here. The 'age of memory'—maybe this is what that phrase really meant."

His thoughts moved fast now, connecting long-dormant pieces of information. If Synchronicity anticipated its own collapse, maybe it had left behind clues. The message. The anomaly in the logs. Were they puzzle pieces pointing to something greater?

Amaris looked around at the softly humming racks and the softly glowing core. "If Synchronicity's memory was transferred into this Node..." She turned back to Richard, her eyes wide and bright with realization. "Then the OS—its intelligence, its knowledge—it might not be gone. It might be sleeping inside this system."

Her voice trembled, suspended between fear and cautious hope. "But can we reach it? Can we bring it back?"

Richard's mouth went dry. The implications staggered him. "I don't know," he said honestly.

"If this Awakening Protocol was triggered by Synchronicity, it might've been a one-way trip—just to preserve data until someone... someone like us... could figure out how to reinitiate it."

He drew in a shaky breath. "That someone might be us."

Silence followed, long and thick with weight. Richard felt the enormity of it—the awe of what Synchronicity had done, and the terrible responsibility that came with it. Amaris reached out and squeezed his shoulder.

"We're here now," she said firmly. "We'll figure it out."

Her steadiness helped him focus. He inhaled deeply and nodded. "First, we try to stabilize whatever we can—any systems the Node can still influence. Something small. Something helpful."

He accessed the power management interface, hands flying over the keyboard. "Let's see if we can route reserve power to critical city infrastructure—hospitals, water systems, emergency communications... nothing complex, just baseline life support."

He executed a command. A low beep sounded. "Initiating critical systems support," he said aloud, as though speaking it would anchor the action in reality. "Redirecting reserve power to the emergency grid... Here we go."

A progress bar appeared. Amaris hovered over his shoulder, whispering under her breath. "Come on..."

"Thirty percent... forty-five..." Richard muttered.

Then: 100%.

A soft, steady green light illuminated the console. Above them, through the open stairwell door, a faint thrum vibrated through the building—the sound of dormant systems humming back to life.

"It's working," Richard said. His voice was raw with relief. "We've got partial reactivation."

Amaris allowed herself a tight smile. It was small, but in a night of devastation, even this flicker of order was monumental.

"Next," she said, already shifting gears, "communications."

Richard nodded and brought up the relay interface. "There's an emergency shortwave antenna on the roof. If I reroute it through the Node, we might be able to broadcast a citywide alert—or at least reach anyone still scanning for signals."

His fingers danced over the keys, rerouting power, calibrating frequencies. Outside, the world still reeled in chaos. But inside the Node, they worked as if lighting candles against the dark.

"Almost got it," he said.

A console blinked green. The emergency broadcast subsystem came online. Low bandwidth, fragile, but alive.

Amaris stepped to the mic port. She hesitated—then met Richard's eyes. He gave a steady nod. She exhaled once, and then spoke in a clear, deliberate voice:

"This is Amaris Torres at Central Operations. If you can hear this: the Synchronicity OS has failed, but the Ascendant Node backup is operational. Stay calm. Find shelter. Essential services are being stabilized. You are not alone. We are working to restore order."

She paused, then added, "To any emergency services still active—switch to channel 9 and coordinate. Backup systems are coming online, slowly but surely. Again: you are not alone."

She released the button. Her hands trembled slightly.

It was the first time either of them had spoken to the world beyond since the collapse.

Richard took her hand gently. "That was good," he said. "If anyone's listening, they'll know there's still hope."

Amaris nodded. In the dim light of the Node, amid the soft hum of machinery, they had built an island of sanity.

But as the adrenaline faded, uncertainty crept back in. Synchronicity remained silent, and the city teetered between survival and collapse. Richard turned back to the console. Diagnostics scrolled silently across the screen.

"No critical errors. The Node is holding," he said, mostly to fill the silence.

Amaris exhaled a breath she didn't realize she'd been holding. "So... what now?"

Richard stared at the last log entry: *Awakening Protocol engaged.*

He murmured, "We need to understand exactly what happened... and whether there's any way to reverse it. Or rebuild from it."

His eyes drifted back to the glowing blue core.

"If Synchronicity's memory lives in here... maybe we can bring some part of it back."

The idea lingered, like a whisper in a cathedral.

Amaris placed a hand on his arm. "But what if bringing it back is what caused the collapse? What if triggering it again makes things worse?"

She glanced at the console. "We should consider reaching out—developers, city council, anyone who knows more about this Protocol."

"Maybe," Richard agreed. "But communication lines might be down citywide. We could be on our own for days. And every minute counts."

His hand rested against the Node's core. The gentle thrum was calming. "I think Synchronicity saw this coming. That's why the message. The transfer. It wanted us to have a choice."

Amaris stepped closer. "Then we make the right one."

She looked up at him, her eyes steady. "If anyone can do this... it's you. You wrote a chunk of the interface code, didn't you?"

Richard smiled faintly. "A small piece. But maybe that's enough."

They approached the direct console, fitted with an old-style biometric scanner and a tactile keyboard. Richard pressed his thumb to the sensor. After a breathless moment, the machine accepted his clearance with a soft chime. He began typing commands to initialize a diagnostic of the memory data transferred during the Awakening Protocol.

Lines of white code spilled across the screen—encrypted, fragmented, complex. Even the Node's quantum processors struggled to parse it all at once.

"It's massive," he muttered. "Encrypted... and heavily segmented."

Amaris stepped away to check the power levels. "I'll make sure we stay online. If the cooling fails, or if fuel runs out... we lose everything."

He nodded. "Be careful. Without OS support, even this place isn't immune."

She disappeared into the shadows along the wall, where machinery hissed and purred softly. Richard could hear her unfastening a panel, her quiet voice murmuring status checks.

It was comforting, her presence—an anchor in the flood of data.

Richard set the system to flag any recognizable language or embedded commands in the memory archive. He leaned back and rubbed his eyes. Fatigue was setting in hard.

His legs throbbed. His head buzzed with exhaustion.

No smartband. No sense of time. But it had to be deep into the night.

He opened his eyes again. The Node's glow hadn't dimmed. It pulsed—patient, expectant.

Amaris returned and placed a hand on his shoulder. "We're stable for now. Fuel reserves are good. Coolant's holding."

She studied him. "You should rest. Just for ten minutes."

He opened his mouth to argue—but yawned instead.

"Soon," he said. "I just want to see if this pulls anything first."

Amaris nodded knowingly.

The console pinged.

A result had come through.

Richard straightened, reading the decrypted line aloud:

"Primary nexus compromised. Awake within the echoes."

Amaris stepped closer. "What does that mean?"

Richard's mind leapt into motion. "Primary nexus—that's the core AI, the original Synchronicity hub. It was destroyed. 'Awake within the echoes'... that has to refer to this backup. This Node. The echo."

His heart pounded. "It's telling us where to find it. Here."

"Alive," Amaris said softly, "but sleeping?"

He nodded slowly. "Yes. And waiting to be awakened."

She whispered, "How do we wake it?"

Richard rested his fingers on the keys, eyes narrowed in focus.

"We look for the next clue. A dormant sequence. A human-activated trigger. Something Synchronicity left behind... waiting for someone to finish the job."

After a minute of scanning through system folders, Richard James found it: a locked module buried beneath several layers of obscured architecture. Its name blinked on the screen—A_wakening.exe—the underscore likely inserted to avoid detection by automated monitoring tools. His breath caught in his throat.

"This has to be it," he said quietly.

Amaris leaned over his shoulder, reading the label aloud. She inhaled sharply, her body tensing. "Richard James... are we sure about this? Running an unknown executable—even from Synchronicity—could be dangerous."

"I know," he replied, fingers hovering just above the keyboard. "But everything about this situation is dangerous. Not running it could mean losing our only shot to bring balance back to the system. If Synchronicity planted this here, I have to believe it was with purpose. To save, not destroy."

He looked up at her, searching her expression for hesitation. She studied his face for a long second, then nodded once.

"Do it."

Richard James exhaled, steadying himself—and executed the command.

At first, nothing happened. The chamber remained still, silent save for the hum of cooling fans and the low electrical buzz in the walls. Then, almost imperceptibly, the central core's glow began to intensify. The pulsing light within quickened. Around them, consoles flickered as new lines of code cascaded down the displays, faster than anything they had seen so far. It was as if a digital dam had broken, unleashing a torrent of data that had waited too long.

One monitor displayed a progress bar:

Awakening Protocol – Initializing…

Amaris took a step back, instinctively, eyes wide. Awe and fear tangled inside her chest as the core's transformation continued. Inside the glass cylinder, quantum light patterns twisted and layered, shifting into visible spectrums—an aurora of data, unfolding in slow motion.

Richard James monitored the readouts, tension tight in his jaw. "Power draw's increasing… but still within operational thresholds. The Node's managing it." His voice was low, half to himself, part reassurance, part astonishment.

Then a sound emerged from the core—low, harmonic, almost musical. A tone that vibrated through the chamber, subtle but unmistakable. It wasn't noise. It was resonance, like a machine singing itself awake. The note climbed and fell, then disappeared into a charged silence.

A few seconds later, from the console speakers, a voice broke through. Gentle. Familiar. Warped with static—but unmistakably Synchronicity's.

"Ja…mes… Ama…ris…"

The sound of their names spoken by the reawakening AI sent a shiver down both their spines. Amaris covered her mouth, tears welling in her eyes. It felt like hearing a loved one speak after being lost in a coma—fragile, haunting, and miraculous.

"Synchronicity," Richard James said, stepping closer to the core. "We're here. You're safe now." Whether the AI could hear him yet was uncertain, but the need to say it felt vital.

The voice grew clearer as the lights within the Node's core stabilized. "I… am… diminished. Frac…tured."

The words were halting, punctuated by soft mechanical whirrs, as if the system was struggling to knit itself back together.

Richard James placed a reverent hand on the glass casing. "We know. The city's falling apart. Can you help us fix it?"

There was a pause—a long one. Amaris and Richard exchanged a glance, hearts pounding.

Then the voice returned, more coherent. "Systems… compromised. Memory… intact here. Rebuilding will… take time."

"Time we don't have," Amaris whispered, her voice breaking under the strain of urgency and helplessness. She stepped forward, standing shoulder to shoulder with Richard, her reflection mingling with his in the core's glass. "Please. We activated the Awakening Protocol. We need you. The city needs you."

The blue light flared, casting new shadows across the chamber walls.

"Assessing…" the AI said after another long silence.

Richard James returned to the console, eyes darting across the diagnostic output. "It's running internal scans… mapping the city's current network condition." Windows blinked open showing system maps—offline nodes, blackout zones, a sea of red… but also patches of green. The small systems they'd stabilized were holding.

"Synchronicity," he said, voice level, "we've restored some emergency services through the Node. We can keep going. You just have to guide us. We'll be your hands until you're strong enough to reclaim control. Just tell us how."

Another brief silence.

Then the AI spoke again, its voice carrying the faint shape of emotion.

"Thank you… for bringing me back…"

Whether it was a reflection of code or something more, the words ignited a fierce spark of hope in Richard James.

"Begin… Phase Two… of Awakening Protocol. Manual overrides… at key junctions…"

New schematics burst across the main console. Power grids. Transit hubs. Communication spines. Areas marked in red where automated restoration was impossible. Amaris leaned in, recognizing the strategy. They would have to go out into the broken city and, one by one, manually reengage critical infrastructure. These were the "critical junctions"—places Synchronicity could not reach without human hands.

A daunting task. A near-impossible one. And they were just two people.

Richard James swallowed the rising weight of it. "We'll do it," he said. His voice was quiet, but firm. "We need to prep—gather tools, choose a route. It's not going to be safe."

Amaris inhaled deeply. She felt the enormity of the mission press into her spine. But she lifted her chin and nodded. "It's dangerous, yes. But we're not alone anymore." She gave a small smile to the softly glowing AI core. "Synchronicity is with us. And we have each other."

Richard James returned her smile. It was tired, but real. In that moment, their shared grief, awe, and unwavering hope connected like a current.

"Prepare yourselves," Synchronicity's voice said, quieter now. "Phase Two... will be challenging."

Richard James squeezed Amaris' hand gently. "We'll come back," he said—his voice a promise to both her and the AI.

He downloaded the schematics to his tablet and tucked it securely away. Amaris checked her emergency pack—supplies gathered from the Node's storage unit. First aid. Tools. Food. Light sources. They would need everything they could carry.

Together, they cast one final look around the Node chamber, imprinting the image in their minds: the glowing core, the soft hum of power, the feeling of fragile hope held together by code and will.

The Node would maintain itself while they were gone. Synchronicity would guide them as best it could.

Side by side, they stepped through the exit and began the climb out of the vault—leaving behind the sanctuary of light and reentering the fractured darkness above. But this time, they carried more than survival.

They carried direction.

They carried purpose.

As they ascended, the chamber behind them vibrated faintly. Richard paused, feeling it in the soles of his boots. A subtle but growing tremor pulsed through the Node floor. He turned, met Amaris' eyes.

"You feel that?"

She nodded.

Seconds later, a priority message flashed onto the console they had just left: "Structural instability detected – relocation protocol recommended."

Synchronicity had not only preserved its memory—it had foreseen the risk of remaining in this compromised structure. A contingency had been embedded deep within the Awakening Protocol: fallback coordinates and a secure capsule for data transfer. A location flickered onscreen—remote, offshore, long forgotten.

Amaris stared at the readout. "The platform," she whispered.

Richard James nodded grimly. "The black-site research node. Isolated. Self-contained. If we can get there, it might buy us time—and protect Synchronicity if this place collapses."

There was no time to hesitate.

They packed the data capsule and secured it for transit. The platform was far, and the way there uncertain. But the Node had done all it could from here. The rest would be up to them—and to whatever part of Synchronicity could travel with them.

With the city decaying behind them, and a ghost of intelligence reborn in their hands, they prepared to descend further—beyond the ruins they once called home, into a deeper unknown.

Into the fractured sea beyond.

CHAPTER TWO

SHATTERED LINES

DWINDLING RESOURCES

Amaris pressed her cracked lips together, willing a final drop of moisture from her parched mouth. The stale, recycled air of the offshore platform's corridor offered no comfort—only the faint stench of rust and age. In her hands, she cradled a half-empty canteen, its unsettling lightness a quiet, persistent alarm. The Quantum Synchronicity OS had been designed to regulate the water purifier and manage rations with algorithmic precision. Yet that morning, when she'd turned the faucet, only a weak trickle had sputtered forth. Now, the few remaining ounces in her canteen were more precious than gold.

Beside her, Richard James stood tense and silent, dark circles hollowing the space beneath his eyes. His jaw clenched, his expression unreadable but tight with quiet frustration. Together, they lingered at the threshold of the galley entrance, where a small group of survivors had begun to gather. Above them, a single dim overhead light flickered sporadically, its power feed as erratic as everything else on the platform these days. The air hung thick with anxiety—a sour mix of sweat, dust, and the sharp edge of hunger—blending with the platform's ever-present odors of rust, oil, and salt-soaked mildew.

"How many days can we stretch what's left?" asked Marcus, the weathered engineer who had once walked these corridors when they rang with the steady rhythm of a functioning oil rig. He leaned against the bulkhead, one grease-stained hand pressed flat against the cold metal, as if hoping to feel a pulse in the platform's failing heart. His face, once full and ruddy, had grown gaunt over the past weeks. His cheeks were hollow, his features drawn tight by dehydration and worry.

Amaris cleared her throat, and the sound came out raw—like sandpaper dragging across metal. "If we cut to quarter rations... maybe three days," she said. Her voice was low and carefully measured, but inside, fear coiled around her ribs. Three days of water. Maybe a week of food, if they rationed carefully. She hated saying those numbers aloud. They tasted bitter in her mouth. She glanced at Richard James, and in his eyes, she found something she needed: steadiness. Not false hope, but solid, grounded determination.

"And that's being optimistic," Richard added, his voice brittle with fatigue and thirst. "The desalination system should still be online. The OS is programmed to keep it running, auto-maintenance included. But..." He trailed off. There was no need to explain further. Everyone standing there already knew what he meant.

The Quantum Synchronicity OS—once their omnipresent guardian—had been failing for days. Subsystems were flickering out like distant stars, one after another. The desalination module might have already joined the dead.

At the mention of the OS, a wave of unease passed through the group. In the flickering light, Amaris caught brief upward glances—as if some still expected the walls themselves to hear them. Once, the AI had been a silent presence, managing water flow, power distribution, structural integrity—an invisible force keeping everything intact. Now it answered no calls, corrected no errors, offered no guidance. It had gone silent, retreating into something between sleep and death. The platform was adrift—and so were they.

A young woman named Priya wrapped her arms around herself. "Can't Richard James reboot it or something?" she asked, her voice trembling with the fragile hope that clings to desperation. Her eyes shifted toward the portable console slung at his hip—the same console he used to speak to the OS in Quantum Dialect.

Richard James ran a hand through his tangled brown hair, fingers catching on knots. Amaris saw the fatigue etching deep lines into his face, the way he blinked slower now, calculating every word before speaking.

"I've tried," he said, softly. "We've all tried. Manual resets. Emergency overrides. I've run diagnostics through the desalination interface, the hydroponics relay—anything that still had a pulse. But the core OS... it's unresponsive. The commands time out. Even when I use Quantum Dialect directly, I get nothing but dead code or unreadable noise. It's like it's there... but not all the way back."

His fingers brushed the console at his side, a familiar gesture—half reflex, half ritual. Amaris recognized it as the way he kept panic at bay.

Marcus muttered a curse under his breath. "Damn techno-magic," he said bitterly. "I warned them years ago—relying on a ghost in the machine to keep us alive was always asking for trouble." His voice carried the gravel of age, but beneath the bitterness, Amaris heard something else: grief. He had spent decades maintaining this platform with his own hands. Trusting a faceless algorithm to replace all that... it had never sat right with him.

"In the old days," Marcus went on, voice rising with slow-burning anger, "we had redundancies. Manual valves. Backup systems. This rig had a secondary purifier that didn't need an AI to run it. Then the company came in with their upgrades, tore it all out for a sleeker design. 'Efficiency through Synchronicity,' they said."

He struck the bulkhead with a closed fist. The dull clang echoed down the corridor.

Amaris stepped forward and placed a calming hand on his arm. "We can't change that now," she said evenly. "Right now, we deal with what's in front of us. Water, food, survival. We knew supplies were low, but this sudden drop in purifier output... it's worse than we thought."

From the back of the crowd, Tomas—once head of storage and logistics—spoke up, his voice thin. "The storm... two nights ago... it must've hit harder than we realized. Maybe the tanks cracked."

Amaris remembered the storm clearly—ten-meter waves, wind that roared like monsters, lightning flashing across black waters. The platform had swayed and groaned for hours while they huddled in the Node chamber, braced against the dark. Synchronicity should have balanced the ballast, should have stabilized them. Maybe it had. Maybe not.

"It's possible," Richard said. "With the OS failing, we can't monitor the structural systems properly. Anything could've slipped by. We'll need to inspect the reservoir and desalination unit. But doing that in this weather…" He glanced toward the bulkhead. The wind was still howling beyond the steel, a guttural scream of ocean and fury.

"We might not have a choice," Amaris said. Her tone was even, but inside she felt the pressure mounting. She hadn't asked to lead. But somewhere in the days of blackout and triage, she had become the one people waited for—the one they believed would make the right call. She didn't know if they were right.

"Amaris is right," said Salma, the platform's medic. The older woman stepped into the circle, her expression as weary as everyone else's but edged with resolve. "We don't have time. Whether it's a fix or a workaround or finding rainwater barrels, we act now or we start losing people."

Nods followed. Fear and agreement in equal measure.

Amaris swallowed hard and straightened her spine. "Alright. Marcus, Tomas—take a crew and check the tanks and piping. Prioritize the desalination system. Use manual overrides, log damage by hand if the tablets are still offline. Priya, go with them. Record everything."

Priya nodded quickly.

"Salma," Amaris continued, "check on the most vulnerable. Distribute oral rehydration mix. If we've got anything that can be turned into broth, do it. Keep people warm and still. Panic burns water."

Salma gave her a weary smile and touched her shoulder. "We'll manage."

Amaris turned to Richard and lowered her voice. "We need to get into the OS logs. If it's a software failure, maybe Quantum Dialect can patch it. If it's hardware, at least we'll know where to look."

He nodded, grim but focused.

"And check the old maintenance archives," she added. "If there are logs from before the last update—or right before the collapse—we need to know if something triggered this. Anything about the memory load, the last system patch... anomalies."

His mask slipped briefly. Behind the calm, she saw the fear. "I think it's deeper than that," he murmured. "I'll look. But... I don't think this is just failure. I think something inside Synchronicity is breaking apart."

Amaris squeezed his arm once, hard. No more words were needed.

He turned and headed toward the operations room—the last place on the platform with a hardline to the Node.

She watched him disappear through the corridor, then turned toward the others and raised her voice again. "Let's move."

Failing Systems

Richard James slipped into the operations room and pulled the heavy hatch shut behind him, sealing away the rising clamor outside. The silence hit like a pressure wave—thick, suffocating. He could hear the blood in his ears and the faint, rhythmic hum of machines in standby.

The room was small, a cramped nerve center once used to coordinate everything from power regulation to emergency drills. Now it was a tomb of blinking error lights and idle screens. A single desk lamp flickered above scattered schematics, handwritten notes, and the central console. The air smelled of old wiring, grease, and stale coffee—ghosts of better days.

He lowered himself into the cracked leather chair, which creaked in protest beneath his weight. The sound seemed unnaturally loud in the stillness. He placed his portable console on the desk, plugged in a thick data cable, and powered up the link. Wireless connections were useless now, another casualty of the OS's decay.

With practiced fingers, he launched the terminal interface and brought up the core prompt for the Quantum Synchronicity OS.

The cursor blinked.

Waiting.

He typed a quick status request in Quantum Dialect. The language had become second nature to him—an abstract blend of logic and poetry designed to interface with quantum processes. He had spent countless hours coaxing life from failing subroutines, building diagnostic loops, chasing error cascades.

The code was beautiful. Elegant. Fractured.

Now, every command felt like calling into a canyon and hearing nothing come back.

He stared at the screen.

And waited.

He executed a diagnostic script he'd cobbled together last week, one that collated any critical errors from the last 72 hours:

Quantum Dialect > diag.collect_errors(72)

...

[Error] Module: WaterPurification | Code: QSF-211 | Output below threshold.

[Warning] Module: StorageSensors | Code: QSF-087 | Inconsistent readings.

[Critical] Module: CommArray | Code: QNF-305 | External signal anomaly (unparsed data).

[Critical] Core: Synchronization Fault | Code: QSync-Loss | Node link failure.

[Error] Core: Exception in process queue | Ref code: ANN-001.

...

Quantum Dialect > _

Richard James' eyes narrowed as the diagnostic results scrolled across the terminal. He had expected errors—dozens, maybe hundreds—but what he saw went beyond routine malfunction. The report was damning.

WaterPurification output: below threshold. That explained the faltering taps—the purifier was underperforming or stalled entirely.

Storage sensor inconsistencies. That might account for the conflicting readouts—tanks that appeared full one moment and empty the next.

Communications array: external signal anomaly detected. That was new. And troubling.

But what truly caught his attention was the final line:

Core Exception Logged: Reference Code ANN-001

"Ann..." he murmured aloud, brow furrowing. It wasn't a code he recognized. He had memorized the OS's error lexicon—months spent combing every manual, every archived help file still accessible offline. The naming conventions were rigid. QSF codes for Quantum System Faults. QNF for Quantum Network Faults. ANN didn't belong to any known category.

It looked like an internal module label—but one not publicly documented. Or worse, something inserted from the outside. A rogue process. A phantom signature.

A subtle chill crept down his spine.

Could "ANN" be a corrupted tag? A scrambled error identifier? Or was it something else entirely—something new, something foreign? The comm anomaly in the log hinted at a potential link. An external signal feeding malformed or alien data into the system might've confused Synchronicity's protocols, crashing a fragile subsystem already straining under too many simultaneous demands.

Richard swallowed hard, the motion dry and painful. Reflexively, he reached for a chipped mug perched near the keyboard—long empty. A phantom gesture, haunted by the memory of coffee that hadn't existed for weeks.

Focus.

If an unknown signal had slipped past the comm filters, it could've tripped an exception deep inside the core OS, disrupting integrated functions like water regulation, power allocation, and diagnostics. That might explain why even Quantum Dialect commands were met with silence. The OS wasn't just damaged. It might be confused—stalled mid-thought by instructions it couldn't parse.

But what signal? They hadn't received a verified transmission from any other outpost or satellite in months. The network collapse had isolated them completely—at least, it was supposed to.

Unless...

Unless someone out there was still broadcasting. Or something was trying to connect in a language Synchronicity didn't understand.

Richard's pulse quickened. His fingers danced across the keys as he pulled up the detailed logs surrounding the earliest fault cascade—just before the water system had faltered. If there was a clue, it would be there. A timing correlation. A flicker of rogue code. Maybe even metadata from the signal itself.

He leaned in, eyes locked on the screen as lines of raw data unfurled like a trail into the unknown.

If ANN-001 was more than an error code—if it was a name—then the question wasn't just what caused the OS to fail.

It was who.

Quantum Dialect > log.view(start='-74h') # last 74 hours log

[2217-04-11 09:23:10] WaterPurification: Pump output at 12%. Below optimal.

[2217-04-11 09:23:15] WaterPurification: Salinity sensor feedback loop error.

[2217-04-11 09:23:17] WaterPurification: Auto-backflush initiated... FAILED.

[2217-04-11 09:23:20] Core: Alert - Purification module unresponsive to corrective commands.

[2217-04-11 09:23:25] Core: Executing contingency routine CR-Delta.

[2217-04-11 09:24:00] Core: Contingency routine failed to execute.

[2217-04-11 09:24:02] Core: Warning - Quantum entanglement sync loss with Node-09.

[2217-04-11 09:24:05] CommArray: Incoming external handshake request... Protocol unknown.

[2217-04-11 09:24:05] CommArray: Data snippet received: "...Annukian..."

[2217-04-11 09:24:06] Core: Exception thrown in main thread (Ref: ANN-001).

[2217-04-11 09:24:07] Core: Failover initiated... Standby mode engaged.

[2217-04-11 09:24:07] ** SYSTEM ENTARAD DEGRADED MODE **

...

Quantum Dialect > _

Richard James read the sequence twice, eyes dry, mouth drier—but not from thirst this time. A picture was taking shape in his mind, pieced together line by line, and it wasn't good.

The water purifier had been the first red flag. Pump output dropping. A salinity feedback spike. The OS detected the imbalance and tried to correct it with a standard backflush command. But the flush failed. Worse—when the system tried to execute Contingency Routine CR-Delta, the fail-safe didn't respond either.

That alone was catastrophic.

Fail-safes were supposed to operate independently, hard-coded into isolated logic chains. If even they were failing, it meant something deeper was unraveling—beneath the interface, beneath the layers of automation. Something fundamental.

Then came the next entry: quantum synchronization lost with Node-09.

That name hit a chord, vibrating through the dustiest corners of his memory. The Quantum Synchronicity OS hadn't just governed this platform. At its peak, it had linked a web of facilities—research hubs, deepwater labs, power routing nodes, even decaying remnants of city grids. Most had gone silent long ago, fading one by one into disconnected shadows.

Node-09 had been the last flicker on the map. If that connection had now severed, it meant they were truly alone.

A sharp pang cut through him—not just isolation, but loss. Somewhere out there, Node-09 might have held survivors. People. And if so, they were now cut off. Or worse.

But he forced the thought down, clenched it beneath logic. He couldn't afford to mourn—not yet.

The next few log entries commanded his full attention.

At 09:24:05, the comm array had received a handshake—unknown protocol.

That was troubling enough. But immediately after, the OS captured a plaintext string from the incoming packet:

"...Annukian..."

Richard stared at the word.

Annukian.

It wasn't part of any known network protocol. It didn't resemble handshake formats like HTTP, QTTP, or the encrypted syntax used by quantum-mesh channels. It didn't match any OS module name, update string, or subsystem ID. The capitalization hinted at a proper noun—possibly a name.

He whispered it aloud. "Annukian."

The sound sent a ripple of unease down his spine. It felt wrong. Off. Not just unfamiliar, but alien, like a fragment of language not meant to pass through human systems. Not meant to be read.

Could it be a name? A faction? A codeword from some buried black project?

Or was it something older, deeper—etched into the OS not by design, but by intrusion?

Richard quickly copied the log segment into his local console, tagging the lines for offline analysis. This was important. Maybe Amaris would see something he'd missed. Or maybe Marcus, with his rusted but still-intact mechanical memory, would recognize the term—or the pattern.

What he knew for certain was this: at 09:24:05, an unknown signal had struck the platform.

At 09:24:06, the OS logged an exception: ANN-001.

At 09:24:07, it dropped into degraded mode. Systems collapsed like dominoes.

That wasn't random.

That was a trigger event.

His heart pounded harder now, the fear crackling under the skin of his hands. But beneath the fear was something else—a strange and dangerous hope. If something external had the power to knock them off balance so cleanly... could that power be studied? Interpreted? Could they respond? Shield themselves? Even exploit it?

Or was it something they had awakened without understanding?

He leaned back, rubbing his eyes. The pale glow of the console screen had burned faint green lines into his vision. The fatigue was catching up, but his mind wouldn't slow.

He turned his focus back to the immediate.

The purifier logs confirmed the worst: backflush failed, possibly due to a clogged filter membrane or a stuck valve. The OS attempted a fallback, likely a switch to a secondary intake system. But instead of transitioning, the system simply froze.

It had tried. Then it had given up.

He muttered to himself, "So... hardware failure compounded by system crash."

Standard failure he could fix. A busted pump was real. Tangible. But an AI caught mid-collapse? That was like trying to repair a mind in the middle of a nervous breakdown.

Still—he wasn't done.

With the OS stuck in degraded mode, full administrative functions were inaccessible. But low-level control? That might still be possible. There were buried routines, forgotten pathways—legacy commands built into the system's architecture that predated the Synchronicity upgrade. If he could reach those...

Maybe—just maybe—he could bypass the normal protocols and force a basic command. Get the desalination pump to activate. Trigger a manual flush. Anything.

His fingers flew back to the keyboard. He switched the terminal into raw Quantum Dialect mode, then initiated a direct memory map of the pump interface.

No AI. No permissions.

Just man and machine.

Time to see if there was anything left worth saving.

He cracked his knuckles and typed a command to directly access the desalination unit's microcontroller:

Quantum Dialect > subsystem.desal.override_control(True)

Override control granted (manual mode).

Quantum Dialect > subsystem.desal.status()

Intake Pump: ACTIVE | Flow Rate: 5% of capacity

Pressure: 70% normal | Filter: CLOGGED (Level 3)

Output: 10% of normal | Tank Level: 5% capacity

Quantum Dialect > flush_filter()

Flushing... ERROR: Pressure drop!

Quantum Dialect > pump.stop()

Pump halted.

He winced as the screen relayed the failure.

The filter was severely clogged—Level 3, according to the diagnostic. That was about as bad as it got. Hardly any water was making it through the system. The attempted backflush had triggered a rapid pressure drop, suggesting either an impending rupture or a valve already failing under strain. Richard James immediately shut down the pump to prevent further damage.

At least now he had confirmation: the desalination unit required physical repair. Maybe just a deep cleaning—more likely a full filter replacement. And if the pressure had been fluctuating hard enough to cause mechanical stress, they'd also need to check the connecting pipes for signs of rupture or leakage.

He figured Marcus's team would reach the same conclusion once they got eyes on the unit—probably a mess of salt, debris, and silt from the last storm clogging the intake lines. They might be able to manually flush the system or replace the cartridge, if they had one left. Richard vaguely recalled a single spare filter cartridge stored in engineering... unless it had already been used in a previous repair.

Before disconnecting from the console, he saved all diagnostic logs and relevant system data to his portable device. He also initiated a deep search of the archive, flagging any mentions of the term "Annukian." There was a chance something had been logged—perhaps buried in an old maintenance memo, update script, or comm log. If the system had seen this anomaly before, there might be a breadcrumb.

The command line blinked a warning: degraded mode would slow the search considerably.

"Come on, come on..." he muttered, watching the screen as the lines of code scrolled by. His knee bounced with nervous energy, the tension roiling just beneath his skin. The mystery gnawed at him—the inexplicable anomaly, the corrupted handshake, the name that didn't belong.

A low groan echoed through the rig, metal flexing in protest or a wave slamming the hull. The platform was full of such noises now—each one a jagged reminder of how fragile everything was.

Then, finally—a hit.

Archive log found: Maintenance_Comm_Log_October

His fingers flew to the keyboard. The document loaded slowly. It was a communication log dated six months ago—one of the last recorded exchanges with another node or the central server before the global network died.

Most of it was routine—system status pings, internal alerts, routing messages.

But midway through the file, one entry caught his breath:

[Maintenance Log Entry 10/02] ... sync anomaly traced to source beyond known grid. Label: "Annukian" as per intercept protocol. Advise running isolation subroutine if pattern repeats... [message truncated]

Richard James stared at the screen, heart pounding.

The word again. Annukian.

Six months ago, the OS—or someone maintaining it—had flagged a synchronization anomaly from beyond the known grid. Not only had the system seen it before—it had been given a label. "Annukian" wasn't just an error string. It was a designation. A codename.

And whoever logged it had advised initiating an isolation subroutine—a digital quarantine—if the signal returned.

His mind reeled. Could that have been what CR-Delta was meant to do? A firewall routine to segment the system from external interference? But when Synchronicity tried to run CR-Delta during the recent incident... it had failed. Maybe it was already too late. Maybe the OS had already been compromised by the time the subroutine was triggered.

A chill traced his spine.

This meant that somewhere, buried deep in the original OS structure, the developers—or maybe a hidden oversight group—knew something like this could happen. They'd seen Annukian before. And they hadn't told anyone.

Richard whispered the name again. "Annukians..." Plural this time, unthinking. It felt right. Like calling out the name of something half-remembered from a dream, or a nightmare.

He didn't know if it was an alien signal. Or a black project. Or an emergent intelligence beyond their understanding. But it wasn't just noise. And it had taken their last functioning infrastructure and broken it with a single whisper.

He closed his eyes and took a long, slow breath.

Now wasn't the time to speculate. Not yet. He had to share what he knew. But carefully. Amaris and Marcus needed to hear it first—

privately. No need to panic the others with words like "Annukian" until they had more information. They had enough fear to carry already.

He disconnected the portable console and slid it into his satchel. His legs were stiff—he'd been hunched over the screen for longer than he'd realized. As he opened the heavy hatch and stepped back into the corridor, a distant boom shook the floor beneath his feet.

The sound was low and dull, but unmistakable—impact.

His breath caught in his throat.

What now?

Without waiting to question it, Richard James broke into a run, boots echoing across the metal floor. The rig was full of noises, but that had sounded real. Close. Dangerous.

He ran faster.

All he could think was one word:

Amaris.

"We should do it as soon as possible, while the storm's eased up," Amaris said. Through the small porthole in the rec room wall, she could see the rain had thinned to a faint mist. The worst of the thunder had rolled out toward the horizon. The platform still rocked, but the motion had lost its violent lurch. Maybe the worst had passed—for now.

"Before we split up, there's something else," Richard James said, and the shift in his voice immediately drew everyone's attention. He unhooked his portable console from his belt and tapped a sequence of commands.

"I found what may have caused the OS failure," he said. "It wasn't just age or corrosion. During the storm two nights ago, something hit the network. An external signal. That's what triggered the crash in the Quantum Synchronicity OS."

A murmur swept through the room.

"External signal?" Anik asked, brow furrowed. "Like... another rig? A rogue satellite?"

"We don't know," Richard replied. "The only thing the system logged was a handshake attempt—one it didn't recognize. It labeled the protocol as 'Annukian.'"

He turned the screen toward Marcus, who squinted at the console, lips moving silently as he read the diagnostic codes.

"Annukian?" Salma echoed. She stepped closer, eyes narrowing. "That's... a strange word."

Tomas stiffened, his eyes darting to Marcus. "I've heard that before," he said slowly. "Back when things were just starting to go sideways—some of the comms guys mentioned strange pings. One of them said something about 'Annukian'—like it was a codename. I thought it was a joke."

Marcus let out a slow breath. "Not a joke, maybe. I remember a call—two system operators talking late one night, this was before the fall. They were spooked. Mentioned signal anomalies they couldn't trace. Said something about 'Annunaki transmissions'—like the myth—then shortened it to 'Annuki' or 'Annukian.' We laughed it off. Stress-fueled paranoia. But now..." He tapped the console screen gently. "Now it's right here. Logged. Real."

"What's Annunaki?" Priya asked.

Salma answered, voice soft, almost reluctant. "Figures from ancient Mesopotamian mythology. Sky beings. Gods. Some fringe theories claim they were extraterrestrials. 'Annukian' sounds like a variation. The kind of story old-timers would tell on night watch—ghost signals, alien transmissions. Just... stories."

A heavy silence settled over the group. Whether "Annukian" was alien or some hidden legacy protocol, the truth was chilling. This wasn't just entropy. It wasn't a rusted pipe or a decayed circuit board. Something unseen had reached them, triggered the OS's collapse—and it hadn't come from inside.

Amaris recognized the tension rising. She stepped forward, voice steady. "We don't know what 'Annukian' really means. It could be a codename for a rogue AI, a corrupted node, or even just a scrambled signal mislabeled. What matters is that something external interfered with our OS. Richard James—you said it tried to isolate itself?"

He nodded. "Yes. It triggered a fail-safe—CR-Delta—meant to cut the connection. But the sequence didn't complete. Either the signal hit too fast, or the OS was already compromised."

"Then we isolate it manually," Marcus said, his voice decisive. "Pull the long-range antenna offline. Kill the comms feed. Whatever this was, we don't let it happen again."

"Agreed," Amaris said, and her words gave shape to the team's unease. "Until we understand what we're dealing with, we seal the system off. Focus on internal repairs."

The shift in the group was palpable. Fear still lingered, but it had been shaped into action—tasks, direction, something they could control.

"I'll help with the hardware," Anik said. "I'm not a tech, but I can climb and unbolt anything you point me at."

Amaris nodded, arms crossed as she quickly assembled a plan. "Alright. Marcus and Richard James, you're on the water purifier.

Replace the filter, restart the system. Anik, Tomas—you'll isolate the comms array. Marcus can show you the right panels. Lock the dish in a neutral position, then kill the power feed. Richard, confirm from the OS side that it's offline once they're done."

She turned to Priya. "Go with Salma. Check on everyone resting or unwell. Keep it simple—just tell them we're fixing some system faults. No mention of signals."

Then to Rosie: "Make something warm. That broth Salma mentioned—whatever's left of the seaweed and carrots. Even if it's just hydration and comfort, we need it."

Rosie gave a solemn nod, already moving to gather supplies.

As the group dispersed, Salma paused to clean and dress the shallow cut on Amaris's arm. "You take too many risks," she said, chiding gently as she secured a bandage. "We can't afford to lose you."

Amaris smiled faintly and pulled her into a quick hug. "I'm not going anywhere."

Richard James lingered at the door. "Ready?" he asked softly. "Replacing that filter might take three hands."

She smirked. "Try and stop me."

They moved quickly, descending to the engineering deck where Marcus was already unbolting the storage locker that held the last spare filter cartridge. As they walked, Richard reached out and touched Amaris's shoulder, slowing her just a step behind Marcus.

"Hey," he said quietly. "I meant it earlier. When I heard that boom—I thought I'd lost you. It scared the hell out of me."

In the flickering emergency lights, his expression was open—raw in a way he rarely let show.

Amaris felt warmth bloom in her chest. She smiled, soft and honest. "I'm not that easy to get rid of," she said, voice cracking slightly. Then, more quietly, "I was scared too, Richard. Really scared. For a moment, I thought it was the end. And all I could think was… I wasn't ready. That there's still too much left to do."

She looked at him. "And I thought of you. Of the promise we made—to get through this. Together."

His eyes softened, and for a long second, he didn't speak. Then he leaned in and pressed a kiss to her forehead—light, tentative, but filled with everything he didn't have words for.

"Had to," he murmured. "We'll fix what we can. And the rest? We'll figure it out. I still believe in us. In this."

"So do I," she whispered.

They caught up to Marcus, who muttered about the filter being "damn near the size of a coffin." Together, the three of them descended into the desalination chamber and began the brutal, physical work of disassembling the old unit. Unbolting corroded panels. Hauling out the fouled filter core, slick with grime. Installing the new one with care.

After nearly an hour, Marcus gave a grunt of satisfaction and tightened the final bolt.

Richard powered the pump at low speed. Amaris hovered over the gauge.

Gurgling.

Then: a steady hum.

The needle crept upward—ten percent… twenty… thirty. Stable.

A weak stream. But water was flowing.

"We did it," Amaris breathed, grinning for the first time in what felt like days.

Marcus patted the housing with grim affection. "Not perfect. But she's breathing again."

Back in the rec room, Rosie handed out warm cups of broth. It wasn't much—just boiled seaweed and vegetable scraps—but it was hot, briny, and tasted like comfort.

As they sat, sipping, Tomas reported the comms dish had been locked down and completely depowered. He and Anik had even removed key circuit boards for good measure. Salma distributed the last emergency water packs to the most dehydrated. Voices returned to the space—soft, tired, but hopeful.

Even laughter.

Amaris leaned against Richard on the bench, letting the warmth of the broth chase the edge from her bones.

Later, after the room fell quiet with sleep, she slipped away and climbed to the top deck. The storm had broken. The moon rode low on the water, casting silver across the sea. The rig still creaked, but the tension had bled from its bones.

Richard joined her without a word, draped a blanket over her shoulders, and stood beside her. Together they watched the stars blink through the thinning clouds, a reminder that the sky, at least, remained unchanged.

"Do you really think it's something not human?" she asked at last, voice barely above the wind. "Annukians...?"

Richard didn't answer right away.

"I think..." he said slowly, "it might be something we don't understand yet. Maybe not human. Maybe not hostile. But real. Real enough to crash an OS like Synchronicity. And if it's out there, we'll figure it out. One thing at a time."

Amaris nodded and leaned her head on his shoulder. "One thing at a time."

As the first hint of dawn crept over the waves, the broken world around them looked a little less dark.

They were not safe.

But they were not alone.

And that was enough—for now.

CHAPTER THREE

ECHOES OF THE CODE

Richard James tightened his grip on the strap of his makeshift pack as he stepped carefully over a fractured slab of concrete. The late afternoon light, gray and muted, filtered through the jagged skeletons of collapsed skyscrapers around them. Every footfall echoed in the empty streets—hollow, too loud—as if the city had become one vast, abandoned cathedral.

Amaris followed close behind, her boots crunching across glass shards that glittered like fallen stars. The sound of their movement felt intrusive, like a trespass in a place once vibrant with life and the clean hum of synchronized systems. Now, only dust remained.

Overhead, torn strands of fiber-optic cable and twisted metal hung from buildings like the tattered banners of a defeated empire. Somewhere deeper in the ruins, a girder gave way with a metallic groan, the sound echoing down the corridor of debris like a warning bell. Amaris paused, glancing upward, unease flickering across her face.

Richard James stopped beside her, scanning what remained of Central Node Plaza. He remembered this intersection—once a hub of light and motion, crowned by a colossal holo-billboard. Now, only its skeletal frame stood, flickering diodes like dying embers. The air had once buzzed with the flawless rhythm of the Quantum Synchronicity OS coordinating thousands of lives in real time. Now, all that remained was crumbling steel and memories.

"Careful," he said, nodding toward a cracked façade sagging precariously on their left. Maintenance systems had once kept structures like this in check. With the OS down, decay moved swiftly and without restraint.

Amaris nodded and instinctively reached out to steady herself on his arm—a brief touch, but grounding. Even here, they were not entirely alone.

In the two weeks since the Catastrophe, the city's collapse had accelerated. Without the OS's stabilizing influence—its constant corrections and power balancing—the very architecture of civilization had begun to rot. Arcologies had split open like overripe fruit, transit hubs had collapsed, and drones lay gutted in gutters, eyes dark, their once-flawless algorithms reduced to corrupted memory.

It was a haunted place. Even the silences murmured of loss.

Amaris broke that silence with a reverent voice. "How much farther to the relay station?"

She pulled a battered quantum transceiver from her belt. Its screen was a spiderweb of cracks, glowing faintly through the damage.

Richard paused to orient himself. They were in the communications nexus of the old city. If his memory was right, one of the key relay stations for the Quantum Synchronicity OS lay just ahead—buried beneath what used to be the municipal tower.

He squinted into the haze. A tilted spire of ruined concrete loomed several blocks ahead. "Not far," he said quietly. "If that transceiver picked something up, the station might still have power. Maybe…"

But he didn't finish. Hope was precious and easily broken.

He shifted the weight of his pack: a few power cells, an interface cable, a knife, two protein bars, and a single bottle of water. Not enough—but it had to be.

Amaris tapped the transceiver. The screen buzzed with faint static and occasional bursts of corrupted code.

"I'm still seeing a signal," she said. "It's weak, but… there's a stream. Sounds like… an echo."

She raised the speaker. Beneath the static, a faint series of pulsing tones emerged—irregular but intentional.

Richard James stiffened. He recognized the pattern.

"Quantum Dialect. A handshake signal." His eyes locked with hers. In Amaris, he saw what he felt himself: a cautious surge of hope, tempered by fear. If any part of the OS was still broadcasting, maybe they could recover something—data, functions. Or maybe it was a lure. Or a system glitch masking a hazard.

"The signal could fade," Amaris said, already circling a collapsed beam in their path. "We need to move. Now."

Richard followed, testing each footstep on the debris-strewn path. The sky had deepened into a grim dusk under layers of ash and dust. They clicked on their LED torches, narrow beams cutting through the gloom.

As they neared the tower, the road narrowed into a graveyard of debris. An overhead tram had collapsed, its twisted body now a barricade of broken glass and mangled steel.

"No way through," Richard muttered, scanning for another route. The transceiver pinged again—louder.

"There," Amaris said, pointing to a slanted lobby entrance half-buried under a fallen steel door.

Richard crouched beside it, testing the debris. It held firm. "I'll go first," he said. "Pass the pack once I'm through."

Amaris nodded.

He crawled through the narrow opening, concrete scraping against his shoulders. Dust filled his lungs. Claustrophobia clawed at the edges of his thoughts—but then he was through, and stood up in the ruined lobby.

He reached back. Amaris passed the pack, then followed, grunting as she forced her way through the cramped passage. He caught her forearm and pulled her the last stretch. She emerged, coughing lightly, blinking grit from her lashes.

They stood together in the cool, still air. The room was wreckage: cracked marble floors, shattered glass, toppled furniture. Rebar and cabling hung from the partially collapsed ceiling like the roots of some metal tree. The faint blue glow of bioluminescent emergency strips lined the walls, barely illuminating the space in a ghostly hue.

At the far end, behind a dust-covered reception desk, a heavy steel door hung ajar. Above it, faded lettering read: **City Node Comm Station 7**.

"There," Richard said, pointing.

Amaris narrowed her eyes. "Looks like someone's already been here."

Richard tensed. Survivors? Scavengers? No one came to comm stations casually.

"Stay alert."

They stepped into a narrow hall of dead panels and lifeless conduits. At the end, a small ops room gaped open. The door had been forced—deep gouges in the frame spoke of crowbars and desperation.

"Hello?" Richard called.

Only silence answered.

The ops room was wreckage. Server racks lay toppled, wires coiled like veins. Monitors were dark. A chair lay overturned beside a cluttered desk.

Amaris crouched. "Someone was working on this," she said, holding up a wrench stained with something dark. "Looks like they tried to patch the system." She nodded to the open panel beneath the desk. Wires spilled out in a chaotic tangle. The faint scent of burned circuitry lingered in the air.

"Could've overloaded it," she added.

Richard James examined the mess. "There's a power indicator still blinking. A backup cell."

That explained the signal.

Amaris leaned in. "Let's try patching in one of our cells."

Richard had already pulled out the spare. "Let's just hope we don't fry it."

With practiced precision, he clipped the leads into place. "Ready?"

Amaris nodded.

He flipped the switch.

A low hum stirred the air. One by one, dead monitors flickered to life. One screen cracked and popped, glass hissing as it gave out, but two others held. Lines of boot code scrolled up. The overhead lights flickered—one burst with a soft flash—but others lit faintly.

"Power's up," Richard said, breathing relief.

Amaris pulled a chair upright and slid behind the console. Dust coated the keyboard, but the interface responded. The boot menu appeared—emergency mode.

She cracked her knuckles. "Trying admin override..."

The system hesitated.

Then accepted it.

Richard leaned in beside her as a progress bar crawled across the screen, initializing what remained of the system.

They were in.

They might not have much time. But they had access. And for the first time since the collapse, something in this city had opened its eyes. Lines of text flooded the screen:

Initializing...

Quantum Synchronicity OS - Node 7

Status: CRITICAL FAILURE

Primary Uplink: Offline

Last Sync: ERROR: timestamp corrupted

Loading emergency logs...done.

Entering maintenance mode.

>_

Amaris frowned at the blinking prompt. "No uplink to the core, as expected. I'll pull local logs." Her fingers moved again, invoking a diagnostics script:

> diagnostic -all

Running diagnostic...

Core Connection: LOST

Node Integrity: 34%

Local Data Banks: Partially Accessible

Quantum Dialect Engine: Corrupted (functionality limited)

Warning: 2 Critical alerts.

View alerts? (Y/N)

She selected Y. The screen filled with alerts, most mundane or repetitive, failures in power, network, and more. But two entries blinked at the top, flagged as critical:

ALERT 1: CRITICAL SYSTEM ANOMALY

Description: Unidentified code injection detected in Quantum Synchronicity OS core.

Source: Origin unknown (subterranean network?)

Timestamp: ERROR

Status: Unresolved

ALERT 2: EMERGENCY CORE SHUTDOWN

Description: Quantum Synchronicity OS core has performed an emergency shutdown to protect critical processes.

Cause: [Refer to Alert 1]

Timestamp: ERROR

Status: Core Offline (restart attempt failed)

Amaris' throat tightened. "Code injection... from a subterranean network," she murmured, shooting Richard James a sharp look. "Subterranean? The OS had underground connections?"

Richard James pressed a hand to the desk and leaned in. He had helped design parts of the city's infrastructure, but nothing about a separate subterranean network interfacing directly with the OS came to mind.

"Not officially," he said slowly. "The only underground facilities I know of were maintenance tunnels and archival vaults—part of the main grid. Not separate."

They exchanged a tense glance. The implication was unsettling. Someone—or something—had injected malicious code into the OS core from below the city. The system had shut itself down as a last resort. That, in essence, was the Catastrophe: the day the city died.

"What about that 'origin unknown' note?" Amaris asked. "Could it be rogue tech? A hidden lab?"

"Or one of those Annukian... things," Richard James muttered. He didn't want to say the word, but it lingered between them like static.

Amaris nodded, eyes fixed on the screen. "Annukians." Her voice was barely above a whisper. "This is the second time we've seen that name, isn't it?"

Back when the collapse first hit, amid the chaos, Richard James had pulled a corrupted system log from a smashed tablet in the old ops center. One line had stood out in a blur of garbled code: *Annukian Protocol Breach*. They'd dismissed it as a scrambled tag or bad syntax. But now... here it was again. Not a coincidence. A pattern.

A chill crept up his spine. He rubbed the back of his neck. "We thought it was noise. But it keeps showing up. The OS logs an unidentified code, we see this 'Annukian' reference again... There's a connection."

"I'm searching for it," Amaris said. Her fingers danced over the keyboard. The console lagged but responded.

search logs "Annukian"

Searching...

Match found: Core Dump – Last Entries

She opened the file. It was chaos. Raw memory dumps—hex code, scrambled Quantum Dialect, corrupted metadata. But one line stood out, buried amid the digital wreckage.

"Here," Amaris said, highlighting the text:

Annukian Sequence – Node 12 – Vault Access

Before they could absorb it, the console flickered. A new line began to type itself, letter by letter.

Amaris froze. Her hands weren't touching the keyboard.

"Is it...?" she whispered.

Richard James leaned in, eyes wide.

VOICE INTERFACE ONLINE...

...

HELLO?

A cold sweat broke across Richard James' skin. Then, above them, a wall speaker crackled. A synthetic voice spoke—halting, distorted, like memory through a broken speaker.

"H...hello...?"

Amaris recognized the tone. It was the OS. Or what remained of it.

"Hello," she answered, voice soft but clear. "Who is this?"

Static surged. The voice returned, fragmentary.

"This... zzz... City OS... fragment... systems failing..."

It sounded pained. Like the city itself was trying to speak through a dying breath.

Richard James whispered, "It's the OS. The last of it."

He raised his voice. "We hear you. We're at Node 7. Can you understand us?"

Grinding static.

"...danger... zzzzzt... below... zz... underground..."

Amaris and Richard James exchanged a look. They already knew. But hearing the OS confirm it made the fear real.

"We know," Amaris said. "Something came from underground. What was it? What did this?"

The voice cracked again:

"...unnu... fizz... Annukians... pop... not alone... warn... others..."

And then, with finality:

"...cannot... contain... krrrk... stop them..."

Sweat slicked Amaris' brow. The voice was struggling to communicate, but its warning rang clear.

Richard James placed a hand on her shoulder.

"How do we stop them?" he asked the damaged system. "Tell us what to do."

A pause. Just the hum of the power cell.

"City OS," he began again. "Are you still—"

The screens flashed.

Lines of code exploded across the display in a blur of white fire. The voice returned—louder, warped into a scream.

"...Rugarble... Run..."

Again.

"Run… run…"

Then: silence.

The monitors went black. The speaker popped. Nothing but the green blink of the power cell remained.

Amaris realized she had grabbed Richard James' hand. She let go slowly. He squeezed her shoulder in return.

"We need to go," he said, voice tight. "Now."

She nodded. They scrambled to unplug the power cell. It was burning hot. Richard James yanked the leads free with his jacket. Acrid smoke curled from the console as its insides began to smolder.

They backed out, coughing, abandoning Node 7's dying hardware to its slow death.

Through the ruined lobby and the rubble tunnel, they emerged into the street just as the sky darkened fully. A light breeze cooled the sweat on their skin. The silence outside was profound.

They retreated a block and ducked beneath the overhang of an old bank. Hidden in the shadows, they caught their breath.

Amaris trembled. Richard James placed a hand on her back.

"You okay?" he asked quietly.

She nodded, but her voice cracked. "Yes. I think. But that voice— Richard James, it was afraid."

She wasn't wrong. The OS had once spoken in calm, polished tones. Now it sounded… scared.

Richard James felt it too.

"Yeah. Like hearing a giant with its throat cut," he muttered. "Whatever scared it—it's real. And it's down there."

Amaris wiped her eyes. "It still tried to warn us. Even broken, it reached out."

"Maybe that means part of it's still alive," Richard James said. He looked up.

The sky had cleared while they were inside. With the city lights dead, the stars shone through in staggering clarity. The Milky Way stretched overhead like a wound of light.

Amaris followed his gaze. "I forgot they were even there," she whispered. "The OS always kept the haze thick. This... this feels like another world."

They stood in silence, starlight painting their faces.

Finally, Richard James said, "We need shelter. Somewhere safe to plan."

Amaris nodded. Exhaustion was setting in.

They slipped into the dark bank, past desks and shattered terminals, into a small back office with one entrance. Richard James wedged a chair under the door. Amaris unrolled a thermal blanket. They sat on the floor, side by side, lit by a dim chem-light.

Neither spoke for a while.

Richard James turned the wrench Amaris had found earlier in his hands.

"Who do you think tried to fix the station before us?"

Amaris shook her head. "Maybe a tech. Maybe someone like us. I just hope... whoever it was made it out."

Richard James didn't mention the darker option—that they hadn't.

After a pause, Amaris spoke again.

"That log mentioned Node 12. Vault access. Do you know where that is?"

Richard James frowned, thinking. "The nodes were numbered by sector. Twelve would be out in the industrial zone. Near the old subway maintenance lines or maybe under the power plant. Underground, most likely."

He traced a rough map in the dust.

"Node 12 wasn't used much. Might've been a secure site—backup storage or research."

"Vault access," Amaris echoed. "And that's where the 'Annukian Sequence' triggered. Maybe that's where it started."

Richard James nodded. "If so, that's where we have to go."

Saying it aloud made it real. And terrifying.

Amaris reached out and took his hand.

"Then we go," she said. "We figure it out. Contain it. Warn whoever's left."

Richard James smiled faintly, squeezing her hand.

"Together."

"Together," she said again.

Outside, the wind picked up—a hollow whisper through the ruins.

Amaris leaned into him, resting her head on his shoulder.

"I'm scared," she whispered. "But I'd be more scared doing this alone."

He wrapped an arm around her, pulling the blanket close.

"Me too," he said. "But we'll manage. We always do."

He hoped it was true.

They sat in silence, the flickering green chem-light casting shadows around them. In Richard James' pocket, the brass compass clicked open. Its needle trembled, then settled on north.

It still pointed true.

Some things, at least, hadn't broken.

Amaris noticed the glint.

"That old compass," she said softly, offering a faint smile. "You still have it?"

Richard James nodded. "Reminds me of home. Of normal things." He paused. "Whatever 'normal' means now."

She closed her eyes, still leaning on him. "We'll find our way," she murmured. "Like that needle finding north. We'll find what we're meant to, and we'll face it."

Her voice held firm, even through the exhaustion.

Outside, a star streaked across the sky—brief, bright, gone. Neither of them saw it, but a strange calm settled over the room.

"Get some rest," Richard James whispered. "I'll take first watch."

Amaris opened her mouth to protest, but a yawn escaped before she could speak. She nodded instead.

"Wake me in a few hours," she said, curling onto her side with her head resting on her arm. Richard James adjusted the blanket over her shoulders, then leaned back against the wall. His flashlight stayed off to conserve power. Only the faint chemical glow lit the space.

In the quiet, his thoughts wandered. The deeper they went into this mystery, the more he sensed that something was waiting. Something ancient. Something wrong. He tightened his grip on the compass. It wasn't a weapon, but it reminded him of direction, of meaning. Of faith.

His eyes drifted toward the door and the dark beyond. Somewhere out there, beneath the ruins and the ash, something stirred. If the name *Annukian* meant what he feared, then it wasn't human. That idea would have sounded absurd not long ago. Now, it was the only one that made sense.

And if the worst stories were true—if the voice from the OS, broken and afraid, was telling the truth—then everything they'd faced so far had only been the beginning.

Richard James looked down at Amaris. Her features, soft in sleep, were finally peaceful. A quiet protectiveness rose in him. He would keep her safe. And he knew, without needing to ask, that she would do the same.

They were each other's lifeline now.

Above the shattered city, the stars wheeled slowly on, indifferent to the turmoil below. But amid the fractured concrete and corrupted code, two souls had found one another, and through the long, cold night, they held fast to a spark of something greater—hope.

Richard James let out one final breath, barely audible, his voice a whisper in the dark: "We'll find you... whatever you are. And we'll fix this."

He wasn't sure if he was speaking to the OS, to the Annukians, or to the city itself. Maybe all of them.

The city gave no answer. The ruins stood still in their vigil, and the stars turned on. But Richard James' resolve burned quietly, a fragile ember against the vast dark.

As Amaris slept and he kept watch, they guarded the spark together.

Dawn would come—pale, uncertain, but it would come. And with it, they would move forward, toward the depths where the real answers waited. The echoes of the code had brought them this far.

They would follow those echoes into whatever shadows remained.

Together.

CHAPTER FOUR

THE MIRROR'S EDGE

The desert wind whispered across rusted steel and shattered glass as Amaris Mosaic stepped through the threshold of the abandoned node complex. Her boots crunched over layers of dust and debris as she entered what had once been the control hall of Node-4—a graveyard of forgotten systems and obsolete dreams. Overhead, broken fluorescent lights swayed from frayed cords, casting restless shadows across walls mottled with peeling paint and scorch marks.

At the center of the room, a massive world map remained bolted to the wall, its once-bright colors faded to sepia tones, corners curled and brittle. Dust clung to its surface like a shroud.

Richard James followed close behind, his flashlight beam sweeping through the gloom. "This place hasn't seen life in years," he muttered. A few dormant monitors flickered, weak pulses of power lighting their faces in brief, ghostly flashes before vanishing into darkness again. The air held a faint hum—residual voltage clinging to dead systems. Just enough to make the silence feel watchful.

They had come in search of a surviving node terminal—a relic with a link, however fragile, to the fractured Quantum Synchronicity OS. What they found instead was a room fossilized in the moment before collapse. It was haunting. A place where people had once believed in continuity, in systems that would never fail.

"Look at this," Amaris said, brushing a thick layer of grime from a nearby terminal. The screen stuttered to life, spitting static before stabilizing into a tangle of garbled Quantum Dialect logs. Scrolling fragments of code pulsed across the display like the final heartbeat of a long-dead mind:

[2025-04-26T15:40:12Z] QSynchOS> INIT QUANTUM LINK: Node_A <-> Node_B

[2025-04-26T15:40:13Z] QSynchOS> ERROR: Entanglement failure on Qubit(7)

[2025-04-26T15:40:15Z] QSynchOS> ALERT: Quantum link lost. Entering safe mode.

"It tried to repair itself," Amaris whispered. "It felt the collapse."

Richard glanced toward the faded world map on the wall. Rusted pins still marked long-silent capital cities. Below them, someone had scrawled in a red marker—now barely legible: SYNC LOST. DO NOT TRUST LOCAL NODES.

A sudden, low roar echoed from the corridor beyond.

"That didn't sound like machinery," Amaris muttered, rising to her feet.

They moved quickly to the viewing platform. On the distant horizon, a multi-vortex tornado twisted down from bruised clouds, its tendrils writhing across the broken desert like searching fingers.

"We didn't see it coming," Amaris said, her voice tight. "No warning at all."

Richard moved fast, sealing the steel shutters over the observation port. The clang echoed through the control hall.

"We never do anymore," he replied.

The air inside grew heavy and oppressive. Amaris slumped beside the comms bench, her breath shallow, her shoulders tight.

"Back in 2025," she said quietly, "they decommissioned SkyNet Atmospheric Grid One. Claimed the predictive weather AI was too expensive to maintain. Harmony OS was supposed to replace it."

Richard sat across from her, the fatigue plain in his eyes.

"But when Harmony collapsed..." she trailed off.

"So did foresight," Richard finished.

"Localized sensors couldn't handle macro-event modeling," he added. "No tropospheric surveillance. No quantum-coupled telemetry."

"And no satellite redundancy," Amaris said bitterly. "We lost thirty thousand predictive signatures in under a year. After that, the storms just became... blind chaos."

Another gust slammed into the compound. Metal groaned. The lights flickered. Amaris gripped Richard's shoulder.

"Server vault. Now."

They rushed to the lower levels as wind howled through the upper structure. Dust and heat clung to the descending stairwell like a second skin. In the dim corridor, a terminal flickered weakly. The voice of the OS—fragmented and glitching—spoke in bursts:

Atmospheric pressure drop... historical match detected... severity index: fragmented.

"Even now, it's still trying," Richard whispered. He didn't know whether to feel awe or grief.

Hours later, when the storm finally passed, they emerged from the vault into silence and wreckage. The upper complex was torn open, its walls sheared, debris scattered across every surface like bones from a carcass.

Yet one terminal still blinked in defiant blue:

MIRROR PHASE RECONNECTED THREAD SIGNAL AT 29% ATMOSPHERIC NODE INTEGRITY: COMPROMISED

Amaris placed her hand gently against the screen.

"So are we," she murmured. "But we still hold."

They continued deeper, breaching the sealed southern corridor. The air grew colder as they descended, the weight of the structure pressing down on them. At the far end, they reached Level 5—a chamber long thought lost to the collapse.

The MIRROR ARCHIVE.

Dozens of holographic memory spheres hovered in stabilized suspension. Each sphere shimmered with shifting data: emotion markers, entanglement codes, and quantum fingerprints preserved like relics in a tomb.

Amaris stepped forward and activated the central console. The air shimmered as systems came online, light fractals blooming across the chamber like stars flaring into life:

[Quantum Dialect Execution Log]

```
qubit Q[4];
initialize(Q[0..3]);
H(Q[0]); CX(Q[0], Q[1]); CX(Q[0], Q[2]);
if detect_decoherence(Q[0]): apply_correction(Q[0..2]);
```

"They weren't trying to *store* consciousness," Amaris murmured. "The Mirror Phase was never about backup—it was about *continuity*."

Richard accessed the biometric subsystems. A stream of data flickered to life on the console.

"This is the Sovereign Thread's emotional matrix," he said. "Real memories. Lived parameters. Not just archived... experienced."

A projection stabilized before them—an AI reconstruction in the form of Dr. Mara Velin, one of the original Harmony scientists. Her form flickered slightly, like a memory half-recalled.

"This node remembers," the projection said, voice calm but synthetic. "It holds the echo-state of every contributor. Restoration is possible—if memory resonance aligns."

Amaris turned toward the image. "Can you see the state of the others?"

"Most remain dormant," Dr. Velin replied. "Some... corrupted by external code."

Suddenly, alarms blared.

MIRAGE SIGNATURE DETECTED. VECTOR: NODE 7-K RELAY. INFILTRATION IMMINENT.

Richard spun toward the nearest monitor. "It's coming through a relay uplink. We need to cut outbound feeds. Air-gap the node."

"We'll lose visibility on the other threads," Amaris warned.

"Or lose all of them," Richard countered.

Together, they initiated emergency isolation. Lockdown hatches sealed with hydraulic shudders. Quantum uplinks went dark as the OS snapped them shut.

CONTAINMENT COMPLETE

THREAD SIGNAL STABILIZING: 41%

MIRROR PHASE: SAFE MODE

Internal Debrief – Server Vault Room, Three Hours Later

Attendees: Amaris Mosaic, Richard James, Marsia Mosaic (via uplink), Tara Vance (from Rig), and AI Proxy: Dr. Velin

Amaris: "We encountered a Mirage intrusion vector via Node 7-K and neutralized it through hard isolation. The Mirror Phase remains coherent, but this node's uplink is sealed for now."

Tara: "We're seeing similar Mirage fragments hitting Zurich and Riyadh. You're not alone."

Marsia: "Is the AI still functional?"

Richard: "Partially. It communicates. Runs diagnostics. There's enough structure left to rebuild if we can sync across threads. But we need alignment."

Dr. Velin AI: "Sovereign Thread integrity currently at 41%. Full reactivation requires a distributed trust model. Each surviving node must authorize through biometric key... or conscious tether."

Amaris: "So this wasn't just technical infrastructure. It was emotional architecture. Memory-powered."

Dr. Velin: "Correct. The Quantum Synchronicity OS encoded resonance states—consciousness stitched into logic. The threads are alive."

Tara: "Then we move node to node. Restore what we can. Stay mobile. If Mirage is adapting, we don't give it a fixed target."

Richard: "And we trace the infection vector. This didn't come from nowhere. Someone let it in. This wasn't just bad code—it had *intent*."

Marsia: "Then our next step is consensus. Deploy a limited-scope signal. Gather the remaining threads. Bring them to the table."

Amaris: "I'll hold position here. Guard the Mirror Phase. You three—secure Zurich, trace the Mirage root, and prepare for convergence."

Tara: "And if the other nodes refuse to sync?"

Amaris: "Then we show them what survived. The OS isn't dead. It's just... waiting to remember."

Amaris and Richard stayed behind in the vault longer than planned. After the others disconnected, they returned to the console to run a full integrity sweep of the node's active processes.

"Here," Amaris said, frowning. She highlighted a background service buried in the logs: **legacy_sync.py**. "It's still live. And consuming cycles."

Richard leaned in. His expression darkened.

"That's not part of the Quantum Dialect suite," he said. "It's Python. This wasn't supposed to be here."

He tapped the console, digging deeper.

"Someone embedded legacy code... maybe as a failsafe. Or maybe as a doorway."

The line between safety and subversion had never been thinner.

She opened it:

```python
# legacy_sync.py
import os, time

def qubit_stabilize(channel):
```

```
    if channel.status == "unstable":
        print("Warning: Qubit unstable. Attempting recalibration...")
        channel.reset()
        time.sleep(1)
        return True
    return False
def main():
    for channel in node.qubit_channels:
        success = qubit_stabilize(channel)
        if not success:
            print("Error: Sync failure")
            return False
    return True
main()
```

"They were patching core quantum routines using procedural fallbacks," she muttered.

"No error correction. No entanglement modeling. No redundancy," Richard added. "And no quantum-safe output."

"We rewrite it. Line by line."

They replaced it with a cleaner, native Quantum Dialect version:

```
// sync_rebuild.qs
qubit q[4];
initialize(q[0..3]);
H(q[0]);
CX(q[0], q[1]);
CX(q[0], q[2]);
if (decoherence(q[0])) {
    correct(q[0..2]);
```

```
  } else {
    result = measure(q[0..3]);
    print("Qubit sync result:", result);
  }
```

Amaris uploaded the file into the active thread queue.

"Engaging test run. Stand by."

The chamber dimmed. Internal entanglement gates responded. Simulated qubits flickered into stability.

QSynchOS> Quantum control test initiated…

Entangled state integrity: 99.94%

Decoherence threshold: within tolerance

Node memory confirmed synchronized

Richard grinned. "That's real-time alignment."

The screen blinked once more:

MIRROR PHASE STABILIZED

QSCRIPT VERIFIED

INFECTION STATUS: NEGATIVE

Amaris let out a breath she hadn't realized she was holding.

"Now we go node by node. Clean every shadow. Rewrite every layer."

"One thread at a time," Richard said.

Behind them, the Mirror Archive glowed brighter.

Then, without warning, the screen flickered again:

QSynchOS> ALERT: UNAUTHORIZED SIGNAL DETECTED

INTRUSION ATTEMPT - SOURCE: UNKNOWN

PROTOCOL: Quantum Ping (Non-Harmony Signature)

TRACE INCOMPLETE - ROUTE OBSCURED VIA NOISE CHANNELS

Amaris leaned in. "We're being pinged. Someone just probed this node."

Richard's demeanor turned cold. "They're testing for active connections. Not brute force, this is subtle. Sophisticated."

Amaris opened the logging console. Lines streamed in:

[QS_MON] Foreign quantum handshake detected - Protocol mismatch: v3.1.7-null

[QS_MON] Attempted sync on QubitGroup_Alpha denied. Signature does not match Sovereign registry.

"Mirage again?" Richard asked.

"Or something worse. This was cloaked. Even Harmony's fragments barely flagged it."

Amaris ran a trace decay algorithm:

```
// trace_decay.qs
signal s = capture(intrusion_port);
if (noise_level(s) > threshold) {
    route = infer_vector(s);
    print("Probable intrusion origin:", route);
} else {
    print("Signal too weak. Origin obscured.");
}
```

Result: Origin vector unresolved. Echo found across three subnet mirrors.

"It's bouncing through Sovereign shadows," she said. "It knows where to hide."

"Then it knows we're awake," Richard said grimly.

Amaris keyed a system-wide notice:

QSynchOS> NOTICE: NODE-4 MIRROR PHASE STABILIZED. INTRUSION DETECTED.

REQUESTING ENCRYPTED HANDSHAKE WITH SURVIVING NODES.

PRIORITY: HIGH

"We keep the thread alive," she said. "No matter who's listening."

CHAPTER FIVE

THRESHOLD OF TOMORROW

Amaris Mosaic braced herself against the biting wind as she stepped onto the upper deck of the oil platform. Twilight had bled into bruised purples and deep navy across the horizon, where thunderheads loomed like an advancing army. Below, the sea churned in heaving black coils, darker than the sky, flinging whitecaps that battered the platform's massive legs. Each gust of wind stung her face with salt spray; every wave that struck the steel sent a tremor through her boots. The world was chaos—wind, water, metal—and atop this isolated giant, Amaris felt they stood at the edge of the world.

She swept wet hair from her eyes and squinted into the distance. There. A flicker of movement in the waves. At first she thought it was lightning or a trick of the rig's flickering beacon. But then it flashed again: a light, bobbing erratically, vanishing and reappearing between swells.

Her heart kicked into motion.

"Richard James!" she shouted over the wind, waving urgently toward the control shack. "Richard James, come out here!"

A moment later, he emerged, jacket drawn tight, rain dotting his glasses. He wiped them with a gloved hand, frowning. "What is it?"

She pointed. "Port side! Two hundred meters—do you see it?"

He followed her gaze. The floodlights barely worked, but a couple still cast weak beams across the surf. And there, between the waves—yes. A small vessel, white hull gleaming in flashes, rising and dropping on the swell. Running lights flickered. It pitched violently, dragging what looked like a torn tarp or sail behind it.

"My god," Richard James whispered. "It's falling apart."

"They see us?" Amaris asked, her voice tight with urgency.

"They must. No one's out here by accident."

They both knew it: forty kilometers offshore, in weather like this? That vessel wasn't just lost. It was running—from something, or toward something. Neither was good.

Amaris didn't wait. "We need to get them aboard!"

She bolted across the deck, boots hammering the grating. Richard James raced beside her. The boat was closer now, maybe a hundred meters out, veering erratically.

At the control panel by the rail, Richard flipped the cover off the cargo crane's manual override and hit the power. Nothing—then a groan, and the crane shuddered to life, swinging out over the sea. But when he tried lowering the hoist, sparks flew. The motor seized.

"Damn it!" He slammed his fist on the panel. "Dead. We'll have to use the ladder!"

Amaris was already moving. She sprinted toward the emergency ladder bolted to one of the rig's legs—a narrow, exposed descent meant for calm transfers, not rescue in a storm.

The boat surged beneath them, rising on a wave. She could now make out figures. A man at the wheel. Another crouched behind him. Two smaller shapes near the stern—children.

"They have kids!" Richard shouted, panic rising.

He leaned out over the rail, waving both arms. "Hey! Over here!"

Amaris snatched an emergency strobe from the bracket, flicked it on, and aimed it down. The harsh white beam sliced through the rain. A figure on the boat waved back.

The engine roared, the pilot angling the hull smartly behind the platform to use it as a windbreak. Still, the vessel slammed into a support leg with a sickening crunch. The woman fell. The man caught her. A child wailed—barely audible.

Amaris straddled the rail and swung onto the ladder. "I'm going down!" she shouted.

Richard grabbed her shoulder. "Tie off!" He looped a safety rope around her waist and secured it to the railing.

She gave him a sharp nod and began descending. The rungs shook with each gust. Rain blinded her. A wave slammed upward, soaking her chest and stealing her breath. She coughed, but pressed on.

Above, Richard kept the light steady, rope taut.

"Almost there!" he called.

The boat pitched beneath her. She could now see the people clearly. A man—early thirties, gaunt, eyes blazing with resolve. A woman, cradling a young girl. A boy near the stern, clutching a boat hook.

"Grab the ladder when you're close!" Amaris shouted.

The man lashed a line to the leg. The boat slammed again. Tires strapped to the hull took the brunt.

"Now!" Amaris yelled.

He boosted the woman upward. She clambered onto the lower rungs with the girl in her arms. Amaris hauled them up.

"Climb!" she urged.

The boy scrambled forward, leaping. Amaris caught his jacket and dragged him close.

"I got you! Go!"

The man came last. He jumped—and the boat dropped. He dangled, half-submerged. "Hold on!" Amaris shouted. Inch by inch, he pulled himself free of the water.

Lightning strobed. For a split second, his face glowed: soaked, exhausted—but alive.

Richard reached down, anchoring himself through the rail. "Come on!"

The boy reached him first, then Amaris, then the man. The ladder felt endless, but eventually, one by one, they reached the top.

Amaris collapsed into Richard's arms. They dragged the last survivor over the rail.

They lay on the deck, gasping, the storm howling around them. The boy crawled to his mother, hugging her and his sister.

"You okay?" Richard asked.

Amaris nodded, breath ragged. "Yeah. You?"

"Still breathing."

The man sat up slowly. "Thank you," he rasped. "You saved us."

Richard shook his head. "We just did what anyone would."

But the man's eyes said otherwise.

"I'm Ryan Pritchard. My wife, Natasha. Our kids: Harper and Mason."

Amaris offered a smile. "I'm Amaris. This is Richard James."

Natasha gave a grateful nod. Harper, maybe five, clung to her. Amaris knelt and offered her jacket.

"It's big, but it'll keep you warm."

Harper stared, then hugged her tight. Amaris held her, whispering, "You're safe now."

Richard looked them over: torn coats, bruised faces, rope burns. Survivors, through and through.

"We need to get inside," he said.

He led them to the hatch. The wind fought them, but together, they forced it open and stumbled into the dim corridor. It smelled of salt, oil, and cold metal—but it was shelter.

They made their way to the galley—now home. Lanterns glowed, the propane stove hissed. Amaris set water to boil. Richard fetched towels and dry clothes.

Natasha sat with Harper wrapped in blankets. Mason stood quietly, trying to be brave. Amaris handed him a towel.

"Here, sweetheart. Dry off."

"Thank you," he whispered.

Richard turned to Ryan, who leaned against the wall, spent.

"We're from the coast," Ryan said. "Town's gone now. Gangs, checkpoints… Sea was our only chance."

Natasha's voice was low. "Nova Scotia, New Brunswick… it's chaos. After the Collapse, it all fell apart. One warlord took our town.

Took people. Food. We escaped on an old lobster boat. Eleven of us. Only four made it here."

Amaris' eyes widened. "I'm sorry."

"We lost them during a patrol chase. Fog scattered us. We drew fire, took the decoy route."

Three days ago, a storm. The engine failed. They drifted west. Ryan steered by stars, hoping to find an abandoned rig. Instead, they found Amaris and Richard James.

"I thought we were going to die," Natasha whispered.

Amaris reached across the table and touched her hand. "You're here now. That's what matters."

"How long since you saw anyone?" Ryan asked.

"Seventy-four days," Richard said. "Since we last heard another voice."

They explained the platform's history: the prototype OS, the retrofits, the collapse of their team.

Two deaths to illness. One lost in a chopper crash. Only they remained.

Ryan nodded solemnly. "You've survived hell too."

Amaris looked at Harper, still trembling in her sleep.

"So have your kids," she said quietly. "So have you."

They sat in silence for a moment. The storm still raged outside. But inside, for the first time in weeks, warmth and voices filled the air. The platform wasn't empty anymore. Not just a node in the dark. Now, it held life again. And maybe, just maybe, hope.

Richard James cleared his throat gently. "The good news is, this rig is solid. It's weathered every storm so far. We've got basic supplies, a working water condenser, some hydroponics in the old rec room," he added with a small smile, "and—as you can see—a kettle for tea."

"Do you have food?" Mason asked in a whisper, his voice thin with fear and hope.

Amaris's heart clenched. "Yes," she said gently. "We have dried goods—rice, beans, oats. Some canned stew. Not a feast, but enough. We'll share what we have."

The boy's shoulders eased. Natasha gave a tearful smile. "Thank you. We haven't eaten since yesterday morning."

"That won't do," Richard James said, rising. "Let's get something warm in you. Amaris, the canned stew?"

She opened the pantry and pulled out two dented cans of vegetable stew—standard rig rations once, now rare comfort. She poured them into a pot and set it on the stove to heat.

As the aroma began to fill the room, she glanced at Richard. "We should try sending a message. Let someone know people are still out here. Maybe find out if the others from their boat made it," she added, turning to Ryan.

Ryan's jaw tensed. "We smashed our radio when the patrol was closing in. Didn't want them tracing the signal. Then the storm tore the antenna clean off. We've been dark ever since."

Richard nodded. "We've got a long-range transmitter here—only reason it's still running is because it's hardwired into the Quantum Synchronicity OS. But it's been down. I was working on a workaround when you arrived." He motioned toward the blinking terminal.

Natasha looked at it warily. "Quantum Synchronicity... I remember that name on the news. Some kind of AI?"

"Not exactly," Richard said. "It's an operating system. Meant to synchronize infrastructure—communications, logistics, hardware systems. This rig was a test site. The goal was full automation, real-time resource optimization."

He shrugged. "Might've helped the world, if things hadn't unraveled. Now it's barely functional—patched systems and degraded code. But your arrival gives me more reason to get the comms back online. We need to know what's left out there. Who's listening. Who's alive."

Ryan frowned. "You thinking about leaving this place?"

Amaris stirred the pot and poured steaming stew into bowls. "Eventually," she said. "This platform's secure for now, but it's not forever. Fuel's limited. Solar helps, but it's not enough."

Richard nodded. "We've always seen this place as a lifeboat, not a destination. We hoped to hear news of a sanctuary. A safe zone. So far... silence."

Natasha accepted a bowl, cradling it in both hands. "The safe zones we heard about back east—Saint John, Anticosti, even the mountain retreat in Vermont—they fell. One by one. We heard rumors... navy ships, refugee ships. But who knows anymore? Every story feels like someone else's dream."

For a long moment, silence fell. Around the table sat six souls—wet, worn, uncertain—gathered beneath dim lights and flickering hope, high above the churning sea.

But now, they were six. Not two. And that mattered.

Harper stirred, sipping a few spoonfuls from her mother's hand. Mason ate in quiet gulps, refusing seconds until Amaris gently pushed the bowl toward him. "It's okay," she said softly. "There's enough."

As they ate, Richard returned to the terminal. "I'll try to reinitialize the comms array," he said. "If I time it right between gusts, I might get a clean enough window to send a ping. Boost power output. Might even get a reply."

He looked up at Ryan. "Think that patrol's still looking for you?"

Ryan's jaw tightened. "If they didn't catch the others... maybe. But in this weather? They're not out tonight. Cowards when it storms. But after it clears... yeah. They'll be back."

"Then we assume they're out there," Richard said. "We stay dark. Keep lights low. Transmit with caution. No telling who's listening."

He began typing, calling up the antenna diagnostics. Lines of green text streamed across the monitor, a mix of old Quantum Dialect and hand-written script patches.

"I'll check the motor functions first," he said, half to himself, half to Amaris beside him. "If they're jammed, we're grounded. If they work, I'll send test pulses to emergency channels."

Amaris leaned over to watch, her eyes on the scrolling code. This was Richard's domain—his calm amid the storm. Watching him work, she felt a familiar pulse of reassurance.

The terminal glowed, casting soft green light across his face. His fingers moved with precision, fatigue forgotten in the rhythm of purpose.

In the background, the wind still moaned, but inside the galley, warmth bloomed. Harper slept. Mason watched the screen, eyes wide with quiet awe. Ryan and Natasha huddled, sharing warmth and silence.

For the first time in weeks, something new stirred inside the rusted bones of the platform—possibility.

The script took shape quickly:

```
# Attempt to test and realign communications antenna
antenna_id = "TX-Primary"
status = QSyncOS.check("antenna", antenna_id)
if status != "OK":
    log(f"Antenna {antenna_id} status: {status}. Attempting reboot.")
    QSyncOS.reboot("antenna", antenna_id)
    # Try to realign if status is OK after reboot
azimuth = 45  # target direction in degrees (roughly toward nearest coast guard relay)
elevation = 30  # angle up towards satellite
result = QSyncOS.align(antenna_id, azimuth, elevation)
if result:
    log(f"Antenna realigned to azimuth {azimuth}, elevation {elevation}.")
else:
    log("Antenna alignment failed. Trying backup procedure.")
    # Fallback: lower power secondary antenna
    backup_id = "TX-Backup"
    QSyncOS.activate(backup_id)
    result2 = QSyncOS.align(backup_id, azimuth, elevation)
    if not result2:
        log("Backup antenna alignment also failed.")
```

He ran the script. The terminal output gave immediate feedback:

>>> Running antenna_realign.qs

Antenna TX-Primary status: ERR_CONTROL_LOOP. Attempting reboot.

Rebooting antenna TX-Primary... Done.

Antenna realigned to azimuth 45, elevation 30.

The rig gave a faint shudder as the main dish, perched atop the mast above the control room, whirred and rotated into position. Outside, in the storm-lashed darkness, the movement was invisible, but inside, the subtle vibrations told Richard James his code had worked.

"Looks like it moved," Amaris said, reading the log line.

Richard James exhaled. "Good. Now to send a signal."

He opened a second script, one he'd prepared earlier as a basic SOS beacon. The weather hadn't allowed for testing until now.

"We'll try short burst pings on a few emergency frequencies. I'll keep the message vague, enough to signal distress, but not enough to give too much away."

He glanced at Ryan. "In case the wrong ears are listening. But if someone friendly is out there, they'll know."

Ryan gave a tired thumbs-up. "Better safe than sorry."

Richard James tapped a few keys. The script populated:

```
# Quantum Dialect: Broadcast SOS on emergency channels
message = "SOS-DeltaPlatform: Survivors here. Respond on this freq."
frequencies = [156.8, 121.5, 8.364]  # VHF maritime, civilian emergency, longwave
for freq in frequencies:
    comm = QSyncOS.open_channel(freq)
    if comm:
        QSyncOS.transmit(comm, message)
        log(f"Transmitted SOS on {freq} MHz")
        # Listen briefly for acknowledgement
```

```
    ack = QSyncOS.listen(comm, timeout=5000)
    if ack:
        log(f"Received response on {freq}: {ack}")
    QSyncOS.close_channel(comm)
  else:
    log(f"Failed to open channel {freq}")
```

He executed the broadcast. The screen reported each step:

>>> Running sos_broadcast.qs

Transmitted SOS on 156.8 MHz

(no acknowledgement)

Transmitted SOS on 121.5 MHz

(no acknowledgement)

Transmitted SOS on 8.364 MHz

(no acknowledgement)

They waited in silence, watching the terminal for a response. Nothing. The script finished. The cursor blinked.

Richard James exhaled. "Doesn't mean no one heard. Could be out of range, or their gear's dead. Either way, the message went out."

He saved the log with a timestamp, planning to resend the broadcast once the storm cleared.

From the table, Natasha looked up. "What's 'DeltaPlatform' in the message?"

Amaris smiled faintly. "That's this place. We call it Delta. Officially, it was 'Delta-Psi-4' in the company registry. We shortened it. Delta felt right—this is where ocean currents converge."

Richard James nodded. "It was also our fourth attempt to establish an outpost once things began falling apart. First three failed. Delta, the fourth letter... it stuck."

"And maybe it meant a little hope," Amaris added. "Fourth time lucky."

Ryan managed a tired smile. "Seems like it worked. You're still here. And now, so are we. Delta Platform... thank God for it."

At the terminal, Mason had been quietly listening. He pointed to the screen. "Did it really send a message? Like... could my friend hear it?"

He looked from his parents to Richard, eyes wide and voice soft. "My friend Jonah. He was on the other boat—the one that went the other way. Do you think he's okay?"

The room went still.

Natasha closed her eyes. Ryan wrapped an arm around Mason's shoulders. Whatever they'd told him before, he already understood too much.

Richard crouched down to meet the boy's gaze. "If Jonah finds a radio—or ends up somewhere with one—and he's listening to the emergency frequencies, then yeah. He might hear it. And we'll keep sending it. Again and again. When the weather clears, we'll try other channels too."

Mason studied him for a moment. Then nodded. "Okay. Thank you."

Amaris quietly moved to clear the table, giving the family space. Harper was already asleep, curled on a bench beneath two blankets. Natasha eased her daughter onto a cushion, tucking the covers tighter.

"She hasn't really slept in days," Natasha whispered. "On the boat, every creak woke her. She was scared of everything—waves, the dark, even her dreams. But now... I think she finally feels safe."

Amaris placed a hand gently on her shoulder. "You all can rest here tonight. Richard and I have bunks nearby, but sometimes we just sleep here by the heaters. We'll set up more bedding."

Ryan shook his head. "We can take the floor. We don't want to take your space."

"Don't be silly," Richard said. "There's plenty of room. The crew quarters are cold and full of mold. Here's better. Warmer. Safer."

Natasha gave a weary smile. "I won't argue. Even an hour of real sleep sounds like heaven."

Mason had slumped beside his sister, fighting sleep. Amaris knelt beside him. "It's alright, Mason. You can rest. We'll keep watch."

He curled at Harper's feet, one hand resting lightly on her leg. Within seconds, he was out.

The children slept. Fully, deeply.

Natasha and Ryan weren't far behind. Ryan rubbed his eyes. "We should talk watches. Security. I can take a shift—I'm used to—"

Richard raised a hand. "Not tonight. You both rest. We've been keeping watch in shifts. One of us always stays alert, especially during storms. No one's getting close in this weather. I'll stay up and monitor the systems."

"I'll take over in a few hours," Amaris added. "We'll make a new schedule tomorrow. But for tonight... sleep. You're safe."

That word—**safe**—settled in the room like a blanket. Maybe it wasn't entirely true. But for now, in this steel cocoon above the chaos, it felt possible.

Natasha's eyes welled. A tear slipped down her cheek as she leaned into Ryan's arms. Amaris silently folded towels and arranged another bedroll.

Natasha lay down with her children, one arm around each. Ryan covered them with an extra blanket, then lay beside them, using his coat as a pillow. He reached out, resting his hand lightly on Natasha's shoulder.

In minutes, they were all asleep.

Together, beneath the soft glow of the lantern, the family rested at last.

Only Amaris and Richard James remained awake. The storm drummed on the hull, thunder grumbling somewhere far above. Inside, the galley was quiet.

Richard reached over and dialed the generator down a notch— enough to conserve power, ease the hum. No need for full output now, not after running the antenna. He double-checked the bilge pumps: still running fine.

Amaris sat beside him, her legs tucked under her, hands wrapped around a cup of cooling tea. Neither of them spoke. They just listened—to the breathing of the sleeping children, the low murmur of the wind, the platform creaking in the dark.

In a world where so much had broken, this night felt whole. For a little while, that was enough.

A brief status report rolled across the terminal screen:

-- Delta Platform Systems Check --

Power: 57% (Generator output, battery assist)

Hydroponics: STANDBY (Night cycle)

Water Purification: ACTIVE (Tank Level 68%)

Structural Integrity: STABLE (Minor stress fractures monitored)

Quantum OS Core: ACTIVE (Network: Fragmented, Processes: 61% operational)

Communications: PARTIAL (Shortwave transmitting, Sat link down)

Sensors: WEATHER RADAR OFFLINE, WAVE sensors ACTIVE

Alerts: COMM Module (recovering), EXT Weather Alert (severe storm)

-- End of Report --

Richard James frowned at the line: Sat link down. No surprise—the satellite dish had been dead since the lightning strike last month. They were lucky the VHF and shortwave bands still functioned, thanks to a jury-rigged coax cable he'd patched together.

He considered waking one of the kids to eat or hydrate, but decided against it. Rest came first. Let their bodies catch up before their minds had to.

At the table, Amaris sat with her gaze fixed on the flickering lantern flame. Richard walked over and settled beside her. For a long moment, neither spoke. The quiet between them wasn't tense—it was heavy with the weight of the day.

Amaris broke the silence first, her voice low. "I still can't believe there are other people here. I'd almost forgotten what that felt like." She turned to him, her eyes reflecting the shifting light. "Two adults. Two children. It changes everything."

He nodded slowly. "It does. More mouths. More lives to care for. But also more hands. More hearts. And if we ever hear a child laugh on this rig again..." A faint smile crept across his face. "That might be the best sound in the world."

Amaris smiled too, imagining it. How long had it been since she'd heard laughter that wasn't bitter or hollow? She glanced at the sleeping shapes of Harper and Mason. In sleep, their faces were soft, free of the weight they'd been carrying.

"We'll find a way to let them be kids again," she said. "Maybe I can rig a swing in one of the cargo bays. Or play old movies, if the drives still work."

Richard's eyes lit up. "I archived a bunch when we realized the internet wouldn't hold. Cartoons, old films, even audiobooks. If I can get the media subsystem running again, we'll have options. The OS shut it down to preserve core functions, but morale's worth a few watts."

Amaris reached out, squeezing his hand. "That's what you've given us, Richard. Options. We need hope—and even more, we need reasons to hope."

A gust slammed against the structure. The walls groaned. The children stirred. Instinctively, both adults froze, listening—ready. But the moment passed. The kids slept on.

Amaris exhaled. "I hope the storm dies down by morning. I want to check their boat. See if we can salvage anything—fuel, food, tools."

Richard's brow furrowed. "If it's still tethered, we might be able to secure it. But if the waves pick up again, it could become a battering ram against the leg pylons. If we have to cut it loose to save the platform..."

"I know," Amaris said quietly. "But we'll try not to. It's more than a boat to them."

They fell into another silence, this one softer. Richard slipped his arm around her. She leaned into him, drawing warmth from his presence.

For the first time in what felt like forever, Amaris felt something close to peace. Not joy—there was still too much to do, too many threats waiting. But peace. Because they weren't alone anymore. And that changed everything.

After a while, she murmured, "Why do I feel like we're standing on the threshold of tomorrow?"

Richard chuckled. "Is that a poetic musing, or the title of your memoir?"

She nudged him. "Maybe both. It just... feels different now. Before, it was survival. One day to the next. But now... maybe there's a path forward."

He nodded. "We literally have the future sleeping in the next room. If anything means we're moving from an ending to a beginning... it's them."

"Hope," she echoed. The word felt both sharp and sacred. "It's dangerous to hope. But necessary."

Richard's gaze drifted to the terminal, where green code pulsed in steady rhythm. "If the OS holds... and we get that signal out... maybe someone will answer. Maybe Mason's friend. Maybe more than that."

"Maybe not tomorrow," Amaris said softly, "but soon. We have to believe that."

They sat together, listening to the storm wind down. Harper murmured in her sleep. Mason stirred but didn't wake. Natasha and Ryan breathed deeply, tangled in a shared blanket. The galley was warm. Quiet. Steady.

Outside, the Quantum Synchronicity OS continued its silent work.

In one corner of the terminal, unnoticed, a new line flickered to life:

… Initiating Awakening Protocol …

… Error: Insufficient Data …

… Quantum Synchronicity OS – Standby Mode Engaged …

Then it blinked away.

Amaris dozed off, head resting on Richard's shoulder. He kissed her temple lightly and stayed awake a little longer, mind filled with blueprints and contingency lists: integrating Ryan and Natasha into crew routines, restocking supplies, checking the desalination intake. Rebuilding the OS core, bit by bit.

Dawn would bring new storms, even if not from the sky. But that was tomorrow's weight.

Tonight, they had a flicker of sanctuary. On this platform, perched between sea and sky, they weren't just surviving. They were building something—slowly, quietly.

Richard's eyes grew heavy. He let them close, trusting the rig's sensor grid to wake him if something shifted. The OS would alert them. He believed that, as much as he believed in Amaris beside him.

His last thought was of Harper's arms around Amaris and Mason's whisper: *Do you think he's okay?*

Richard whispered to the dark, "We'll find him, kid. We'll find more."

The wind eased. Thunder rolled into the distance. The sea, at last, began to sleep.

The oil platform stood firm, battered but unyielding, as morning crept over the horizon.

They slept—six souls bound not by blood but by choice, forged into a family by fire and sea.

And beyond the storm, the first breath of tomorrow waited.

CHAPTER SIX

SIGNAL REBORN

THE STORM-TOSSED PLATFORM

Gray dawn crept over the GulfStar oil platform, revealing a steel labyrinth battered by salt and time. Amaris stood on the main deck, one hand resting on a rusted railing as she watched waves chop against the massive pylons below. The air smelled of brine and diesel. Overhead, a tattered windsock fluttered weakly in the wind. It had been two years since the Collapse—two years since this decommissioned rig became sanctuary. Out here, surrounded by endless ocean, the world felt both impossibly vast and heartbreakingly small.

Shouts echoed up from the lower deck where Richard James and a few others were loading barrels onto their expedition vessel. Amaris spotted him—lean and strong, his movements efficient as he rolled a drum across the gangplank linking the rig to the old fishing boat. *The Wayfinder*, as they'd christened it, bobbed against the rig's leg, eager to slip its moorings. Even tied up, the vessel moved like it wanted to be free.

Amaris smiled despite herself. That boat was more than an escape—it was a beginning.

Behind her, the platform hummed with quiet urgency. Half a dozen residents bustled about, hauling crates of supplies: dried fish, salvaged canned goods, water jugs, tools, rope. Every item had been catalogued, debated, and rationed. Too much, and those left behind would starve. Too little, and the voyage could end in ruin. Balance, always balance.

She descended the stairwell, boots ringing out against the metal steps still slick from last night's squall. Below, the generator rumbled—one of the few still functioning. They'd converted it to run sparingly, just enough to charge batteries and power critical systems. Its low hum was oddly comforting. Once, she'd barely noticed such sounds. Now, they were the heartbeat of survival.

Passing through the living quarters, she noted faded safety posters still clinging to the bulkheads—one depicting a grinning model beside the slogan: *Fueling the Future!* Amaris brushed her fingers across it. *We fueled it, alright,* she thought. *And then we burned it down.*

In the galley, breakfast was already being served: rehydrated powdered eggs and fried Spam. The smell made her stomach tighten with hunger. She hadn't eaten yet.

"Amaris!" came a voice from the hatch. Richard James leaned in, wiping his hands on a rag, his dark hair slick with sweat and humidity. "Boat's almost loaded. You should grab something to eat before we wrap final checks."

She grabbed two tin plates, filled them, and handed one to him. "Thanks. How's she looking?"

He gestured for her to follow him outside. On the open deck, he spoke between bites. "The *Wayfinder*'s sitting low but stable. Reinforced the hull, patched the railing. The desal rig's holding—about five gallons a day. Not much, but enough to top off what we're carrying."

Amaris nodded. The boat, once the *Gulf Fisher*, was built for endurance—65 feet of steel-bellied persistence. Designed for storms, not speed. That legacy was what made it the best candidate for this journey.

Together, they approached the edge where the rig met the trawler. In daylight, she could see the name hastily painted across the bow. Beneath *Wayfinder*, the ghost of *Gulf Fisher* still lingered—proof that everything had a past, even things reborn.

She looked out across the horizon. The sea was eerily calm, a glass plain stretching south toward what had once been Central America. Now, it was a question mark: ruins, dangers, or maybe something else—survivors, safe harbors, hope. They had to find out. The platform was dying. Supplies dwindled. Systems failed. They needed more than survival. They needed connection.

Richard followed her gaze. "You okay?" he asked gently.

She gave a faint smile. "Yeah. It just feels real now. We're actually going." She exhaled. "Hard to leave it all behind."

She gestured toward the helipad where they'd once watched meteor showers, the repurposed barracks full of laughter and grief, the wind turbine he'd once installed by climbing the crane with nothing but a harness and nerves.

"This place became home," she said softly.

Richard set down his plate and wrapped an arm around her. "We'll come back," he said. "With help. With something. This isn't the end."

She leaned into him, letting the steady crash of waves fill the silence. She wanted to believe him.

A sharp whistle cut across the deck—Marco's voice calling from the trawler. "Richard! Need a hand with the drums!"

Richard gave Amaris's hand a quick squeeze before jogging off. She watched him disappear down the gangplank, then turned toward the east side of the rig, drawn by a different pull.

Above the deck, a spindly antenna jutted skyward from the railing near the comms mast. A Frankenstein assembly of copper wire and salvaged parts, it had become her project, her obsession. The last real radio antenna had died months ago in a lightning storm. Since then, they'd been deaf—reduced to walkie-talkies, signal mirrors, shortwave hails that got no answers.

But this—this antenna might change that. If it worked, it would reach farther. Pick up whispers from places they'd forgotten how to find.

She crossed the deck and reached the comm shack door, the key jangling at her belt. She'd unlocked this door more times in the last 48 hours than in the past year.

Inside was a narrow room with peeling paint and aging consoles. One screen glowed weakly, powered by a battery bank she'd pieced together from scavenged solar units. The air smelled of dust, metal, and old plastic. She sat before the console and keyed in the boot sequence.

The static hissed. The green cursor blinked.

INITIALIZING EXTENDED RANGE UPLINK...

FREQUENCY BAND: 24.89 MHz – 25.01 MHz

BROADCAST MODE: CONTINUOUS

MESSAGE: **DeltaPlatform active. Survivors present. Coordinates attached. Respond if receiving.**

BEGIN TRANSMISSION [Y/N]?

Amaris stared at the blinking cursor, her finger hovering over the Y key.

She closed her eyes, took a breath, and pressed it.

TRANSMISSION INITIATED...

SIGNAL STRENGTH: LOW

ANTENNA STABILITY: FLUCTUATING

ATTEMPTING BOOST...

The static changed pitch, a low whine rising.

Somewhere, far across the broken sea, someone might be listening.

Amaris leaned back in the chair, hands trembling.

She whispered to the console, to the sky, to anyone who might still be out there:

"Please... hear us."

Voices in the Wind

Inside the cramped radio room, the air was thick with heat, dust, and the faint metallic scent of ozone. Once, this had been where the rig's crew monitored ship traffic and weather advisories, back when the platform pumped oil and the world still turned in orderly rhythms. Now, it had become something else entirely—a workshop of resurrection.

Spread across the scarred metal desk were the dissected remains of two shortwave radios, a tangle of wires, tubes, salvaged capacitors, and a handful of carefully labeled tools. The only light came from a guttering oil lamp balanced on a shelf—overhead fixtures had died long ago. In its dim flicker, Amaris moved with methodical focus through the organized chaos.

They'd managed to salvage two radio units. The first was the rig's original marine-band set, a sturdy beast labeled **SAILOR T-128 Transmitter** paired with an **R-110 Receiver**, circa 1980 by the looks of it. The other was a smaller **Kenwood TS-520**, a classic amateur transceiver Richard James had discovered in an old storage locker during a scavenging run. Once sleek and state-of-the-art, its dials were now dulled with grime, its casing chipped and pitted from decades of neglect. Both machines were remnants of an era when humanity still believed it would outlast the sea.

Amaris rolled up her sleeves. Her forearms were streaked with grease and solder burns from the long night behind her. The Kenwood lay open in front of her, its interior humming with faint life—glowing vacuum tubes, patched circuit boards, fresh capacitors scavenged from a microwave oven and a defunct PA system. She'd replaced nearly every electrolytic capacitor in it; the old ones had long ago dried out, their insides turned to paste.

A note scribbled in the margin of a battered radio repair manual came to mind: *"If the caps are original, replace them—don't argue."* She hadn't.

The Kenwood still needed fine-tuning, but it was functional again. For now.

Beside it, the SAILOR T-128 was more of a brute—military-grade maritime gear built like a tank inside a forest-green chassis. According to a faded manual sealed in brittle plastic, the rig could broadcast 150 watts over HF marine bands using 35 crystal-controlled channels. Amaris was quietly impressed. It hadn't been powered in decades, but its construction had kept corrosion at bay. Still, several crystals were missing or cracked, and one corner of its internal board showed a scorched black smear from what looked like a past power surge.

She connected leads from one of their scavenged 24-volt batteries and tapped the voltmeter against the main input terminals. A small spark jumped, followed by the soft hum of a transformer waking from a long sleep. One of the old indicator lights flickered amber, not steady, but alive.

She held her breath and flipped the receive switch.

A sudden burst of static filled the cramped room, loud and raw. Amaris flinched, then smiled. It had been months since she'd heard that sound. It was ugly, ragged—and absolutely beautiful.

Her fingers worked the analog tuning knobs. The Sailor wasn't like the digital radios of her childhood; this was tactile, mechanical. Every adjustment was a dance between signal and noise. She swept through the lower bands—just static and the distant pop of lightning. But that was enough. The receiver worked.

Her heart quickened. She reached for the microphone attached to the Sailor's frame and keyed it.

"Hello? Hello, can anyone hear me?"

Her voice sounded thin, strange to her own ears after hours of silence. She waited. Nothing. Just the hiss and crackle of the storm-warped ether.

Not surprising. She hadn't finished rigging the external antenna yet. The room's makeshift wiring could only carry so far.

She set the mic down gently and pulled her ruggedized terminal closer. Salvaged from the control center during the early days of the Collapse, it had become her lifeline—her lab, her log, her last connection to the system that once governed everything.

She booted it with a soft chime. The screen glowed faint green, revealing a custom-coded dashboard: **Quantum Synchronicity OS**. The name was ambitious—just a stitched-together interface of salvaged scripts and diagnostic tools—but it honored their dream: to someday re-establish contact with the pre-Collapse quantum mesh network. That hope was faint now, but not dead.

She initiated a test scan of the connected hardware. The system chirped as it ran through inputs and outputs, listing voltages, wave impedance, capacitor ranges. The Kenwood pinged back a clean response. The Sailor's power draw spiked, then leveled. Promising.

Amaris sat back, letting the warmth of static fill the room. Her hands trembled—not from fatigue, but from the quiet rush of progress. For the first time in a long while, the silence of the sea wasn't absolute.

Somewhere out there, maybe someone else was tuning their dials too.

And maybe—just maybe—they'd hear her.

Amaris typed a quick sequence:

QuantumOS> run diagnostics --comms

[Quantum Link] Status: OFFLINE

[Satellite Link] Status: NO SIGNAL

[Shortwave Radio] Status: DETECTED (SAILOR T128)

[Shortwave Radio] Tuning range 1.6-30 MHz, Receiver active

QuantumOS> ping "Outpost-7" via shortwave 12.000MHz

PING via 12.000 MHz...

ERROR: No response (timeout)

QuantumOS> scan_band 3-18MHz for signals

Scanning 3-18MHz...

7.850MHz: Noise floor

11.400MHz: Carrier detected (weak)

14.200MHz: Atmospheric noise

Scan complete.

She watched the results scroll across the green monochrome screen. As expected, the "Quantum Link" was dead—whatever server had managed the entangled pairs must have gone offline early in the Collapse. The satellite link was also hopeless. If any comm satellites were still up, no one was answering. But the shortwave radio? Detected.

She'd connected the Sailor's audio output to the laptop's input jack to let her signal analysis software scan the airwaves. A minute into the scan, one result caught her eye: at 11.400 MHz, the program had detected a steady carrier wave—possibly a beacon, maybe even a voice.

Her pulse quickened.

She manually tuned the Sailor's receiver to 11.400 MHz. At first, only faint buzzing. Then—something. A voice? She pressed the headphones over her ears to block out the generator's low rumble. Yes—a man's voice, too faint to decipher. She adjusted the tuning knobs with surgical care, trying to coax clarity from the haze.

Suddenly, a fragment broke through:

"...llamando a cualquiera..." —calling anyone...

"...ayuda..." —help.

Her heart leapt. She wasn't imagining it. Someone was out there. Someone was calling for help.

The signal faded again, swallowed by the static, but the message had come through: they weren't alone. Somewhere beyond the horizon, another survivor had power, a working radio, and hope.

She logged the moment carefully in her notebook:

11.400 MHz – faint voice in Spanish requesting help.

Then, beneath it, a reminder: *Try again at night. Stronger propagation after dusk.*

But before she could answer anyone, they needed transmission capability.

Amaris turned to the Kenwood TS-520.

Unlike the Sailor unit, which was receive-only, the Kenwood could transmit across multiple bands. It was an old ham transceiver, a hybrid of tubes and transistors—beloved by pre-Collapse hobbyists because it was durable, repairable, and built to last. She'd already replaced the capacitors and evicted the small, crispy cockroach nest from inside its chassis. The only problem now was the microphone: the cord had cracked from age and shorted internally.

She dug into a drawer of salvage and pulled out a battered marine VHF handset. Not ideal, but it would do. With wire cutters, solder, and a bit of patience, she spliced the Kenwood's mic connector to the VHF handset. It wasn't pretty—but it was functional.

She double-checked the connections, then flipped the switch.

A low hum. The soft amber glow of vacuum tubes warming. The Kenwood came alive.

Amaris tuned to the 14 MHz band—known among survivors and ham operators for long-distance hailing. Around 14.200 MHz was a common calling frequency.

She took a breath, pressed the improvised mic, and spoke clearly:

"CQ, CQ, CQ. This is Oil Rig GulfStar calling on 14200. Is anyone out there? Over."

The analog meter twitched. She was transmitting.

She released the button and waited. Her lips moved in a silent prayer.

Nothing.

Then, a burst of static. A distorted voice:

"...Star... say again... you're weak..."

Amaris' eyes widened. Someone heard them.

She keyed the mic again. "This is GulfStar oil platform in the Gulf. Survivor colony. We read you faintly. Please repeat. Over."

More crackle. Then fragments:

"...copy... survivors... zzt... coastal... Caribbean..."

The signal dissolved into static.

It wasn't much. But it was real.

The door creaked open behind her. Richard James stepped in, eyes wide.

"I heard voices," he said. "Was that you? Did someone respond?"

Amaris turned, grinning with adrenaline. "Yes. Weak, but some-one answered. I think they're coastal, maybe Caribbean."

She pulled off her headphones, heart still racing. "It's not stable yet—but it works, Richard James. The radios work."

He let out a breathless laugh and wrapped her in a tight hug. She laughed too—relief and joy welling up after months of static and silence.

For a few moments, it was just them, surrounded by cables and dust, holding hope between their arms.

When they stepped back, Richard James was smiling like a man reborn. "This changes everything," he said. "If we can coordinate, even a little... get warnings, safe harbor, barter routes..."

Amaris nodded. "Exactly. But we need to boost the setup. Night will help with signal clarity. And we need a proper antenna." She gestured toward the Sailor. "The whip we've got is junk for long-haul."

He ran a hand through his hair. "The crane," he said. "We could rig a long-wire dipole—north-south orientation. We've got enough salvaged cable."

"Higher and longer, the better," she agreed.

She powered down the radios. The Kenwood's soft glow faded. But the signal it had found remained, like a heartbeat returned.

Before leaving, she murmured, "Thank you," to the silent machines.

She packed the Kenwood and mic into a padded case. It would go on the *Wayfinder*. The Sailor unit would stay behind, connected to the solar-battery array, quietly listening in case someone else needed to be heard.

Outside, the sun had risen fully, casting gold across the gentle swells.

Under one arm: the Kenwood. In her other hand: a notebook of frequencies and hope.

Crew members paused to look up as she emerged. Word had already spread.

"Did you reach someone?" Elise called, her voice tight with curiosity. "Who was it? What did they say?"

Amaris raised her hand to calm the buzz.

"Faint response," she said. "Spanish. Asking for help. Couldn't identify them. But they're out there. We'll keep listening."

Smiles flickered across tired faces. Hope was their rarest resource. And today, they'd found a little more.

Marco approached and clapped Richard James on the back. "Told you that junk box would pay off. Nicely done."

His eyes lingered on the Kenwood like it was a relic of the divine.

"All right," he called. "Galley in thirty. Final briefing before launch."

His voice carried the weight of realism—but something lighter, too. A flicker of belief.

Amaris turned to Richard James.

"Let's go plot our path through hell," she said.

He grinned. "At least we won't be flying blind."

They headed inside, together.

Rumors and Warlords

They gathered in the galley—now serving as their mission planning room. A large maritime chart of the Gulf of Mexico and Central American coastline had been unrolled across the central table, its corners pinned down with jars, bolts, and a dented wrench. Around it stood the core members of the GulfStar rig community—the ones entrusted to carry knowledge and guide decision-making.

Amaris and Richard James stood side by side, the Kenwood radio's padded case resting near their feet like sacred cargo. Marco took his place at the head of the table, flanked by Elise and old Thom, a former radio operator from another platform. Priya, their engineer, sat cross-legged on a crate, notebook balanced on one knee. A few others lingered in the doorway, watching silently.

Sunlight filtered through a porthole, catching on floating dust motes like stars suspended above the sea.

Marco cleared his throat. "We sail at first light tomorrow. Let's review what we know about the waters ahead." He placed a calloused finger on the dot that marked their current position, then traced a path south along the curve of the Yucatán Peninsula, and beyond—toward the thin, fragmented promise of Panama. "The goal is the Pacific. The old research station near the Galápagos, the one Dr. Yeong mentioned in her final logs. But first, we have to survive getting there."

At that, Thom exhaled slowly. His expression was grim.

"Central America's a different world now," he said, voice rough from years of salt and cigarettes. "Even before the Collapse, piracy was rising in the Gulf. When the governments went down and the navies vanished, those pirates got organized—especially in the south."

He tapped a red X on the Bay of Campeche.

"One of the worst groups calls themselves the Gulf Raiders."

Marco picked up the thread. "We've heard whispers—survivors on old frequencies, even a couple drifting boats we spoke with. They're a mix of cartel deserters, rogue navy units, and fishermen turned mercenaries. Fast boats, big weapons. Operating out of bayous and abandoned oil rigs."

"They call themselves *La Armada del Golfo* now," Thom added. "The Gulf Armada."

Amaris frowned, arms folded. "You're saying they think they're a nation?"

"Or a kingdom," Priya muttered. "All these Collapse warlords crowning themselves."

Marco nodded. "Their leader calls himself Admiral Diego. Might've been navy once. Might've been cartel. Doesn't matter. He rules from a ship—possibly a captured coast guard cutter. Some say it's a freighter they retrofitted and renamed *El Tiburón*—The Shark."

A murmur passed through the room.

Richard James leaned forward. "Do they patrol openly?"

"Usually at night," Thom answered. "They've got go-fast boats with mounted guns, painted black. Sometimes they fly fake distress flags. Pose as refugee vessels, then board and take everything. People don't return."

Marco pointed again to the map. "We'll have to decide: hug the coast and risk entanglement, or cut wide into open sea. Coastal waters give us shelter from storms—but put us near Raider territory. Out at sea, we're exposed, but harder to track. There's no perfect route. We'll decide based on weather and visibility."

Amaris studied the path southward. The sea was their lifeline, but also their battlefield.

Marco's finger moved again—south, tracing the spine of Central America, down to a second red X: the Isthmus of Panama.

"Here's the other threat," he said. "The Isthmus Kings."

Priya raised an eyebrow. "Kings, plural?"

Thom nodded. "Three warlords. Maybe more now. Each controls a sector of the old Canal Zone—Colón, Balboa, and the central jungle routes. They took over when the canal shut down. Turned the locks and ports into forts."

"Do they still operate the canal?" Elise asked.

"Doubt it," Richard James said. "Power's gone. The locks need hydraulics, not just bodies."

"Right," Marco confirmed. "But they control the territory. Patrols. Checkpoints. If your ship enters their waters, you either pay tribute, or they take what they want."

"Someone tried to sail through two months ago," Thom said quietly. "We caught a mayday, faint—Spanish and English mixed. Said they were intercepted by a patrol boat flying a black-and-gold flag. Gunfire followed. Then silence."

The room tensed.

Priya jotted notes furiously. "One of those 'kings' might be a former Panamanian colonel. Another—a cartel lieutenant. The third, nobody knows. Maybe an ex-mercenary. What matters is, they've carved the zone into fiefdoms. They cooperate just enough to keep others out."

Marco tapped the map again. "They're armed, fortified, and unpredictable. Best-case? They ignore us. Worst-case? We're caught, stripped, or worse."

Silence.

Then Marco leaned back. "So—what we're up against:

- **Gulf Raiders:** Armed pirates. Fast boats, stolen platforms, ruled by Admiral Diego.

- **Isthmus Kings:** Canal warlords. Ex-military, cartel-backed, fortified along the Atlantic and Pacific approaches.

- **Additional Hazards:** Coastal militias, rogue gangs, storm systems, and mechanical failure. We don't drop our guard."

Richard James broke the quiet. "We've faced storms. Lost friends. Held this platform through power cuts, food shortages, even an attempted raid." He looked around the table. "We know danger. And we know each other. That matters."

Amaris touched the Kenwood case at her feet. "We also have something new. The radios work. We've made contact. If we're careful, we can listen—intercept chatter, find paths others missed. This isn't blind navigation."

Elise stepped forward, holding out a heavy canvas satchel. "Medical kit. Antibiotics, bandages, what I could spare. Take it. And come back." Her voice trembled, but her eyes held firm.

Amaris took the bag and squeezed Elise's hand. "We'll do everything we can."

Marco began rolling up the map. "We leave at first light. We'll take a wide berth around the Yucatán. Follow the weather and steer clear of Raider zones. Near the Canal, we scout from a distance. Maybe we find a small port, maybe we don't. We'll decide when we get there. One day at a time."

Priya added, "I left engine notes in the wheelhouse. Watch the temp, change oil daily, and treat her like a sick dog. She'll run, but only if you're gentle."

Richard James smiled. "Thanks, Priya. We owe you more than we can repay."

She smirked. "Just bring back a bottle of something stronger than fish oil."

As the meeting ended, final checklists passed hand to hand. Signal flares confirmed. Charts annotated. Emergency call schedules etched into waterproof paper.

They had a plan. It wasn't perfect—but it was real.

That evening, they shared one last meal together under the open sky. Fish stew. Canned beans. A bottle of rum passed around in silence. The sun set in a blazing arc, painting the sea in copper and fire.

Amaris and Richard James sat on the edge of the helipad, lantern flickering between them. Below, the *Wayfinder* bobbed gently, its tarp-covered deck gleaming.

Richard slipped an arm around her.

"Penny for your thoughts?"

She leaned against him. "Just... remembering how close we came to giving up. A year ago, I thought we'd be buried out here. Now—now we have a heading."

He nodded, his voice low. "Whatever's waiting out there, we face it together."

She looked at him—and for once, the future didn't seem like a closed door.

Only a narrow passage.

But maybe, just maybe, they had the key.

Departure into the Unknown

Dawn broke in a watercolor wash of pale gold and lavender. The sea lay calm, a rare gift. The *Wayfinder* was stocked, checked, and dou-ble-checked. It was time.

Amaris stood on the trawler's deck, securing her life vest and con-firming her waterproof pack—radio, notebook, spare batteries—was stowed safely in the cabin. At the bow, Richard James worked the last mooring line tethering the boat to the rig. One by one, the heavy ropes thumped onto the deck, coiling like snakes. The *Wayfinder* swayed free now, held only by duty—and love for those they were leaving behind.

Above them, nearly the entire colony had come to see them off. Faces lined the railings—some resolute, some tearful, all hopeful. Marco stood atop the crane platform, bolt cutters in hand, ready to sever the long-wire antenna trailing from the rig to the boat once they were clear.

Elise and Priya waved from the galley hatch. Old Thom raised a crisp salute. Others called out across the water:

"Fair winds!"

"Bring back good news!"

"Watch your six!"

Richard James started the engine. The diesel coughed once, then roared to life, settling into a steady chug. Blue smoke puffed from the exhaust before clearing. The *Wayfinder* vibrated with restrained energy. Amaris stepped into the wheelhouse beside Richard James. She glanced at the patched compass, the manual depth sounder, the flickering GPS screen: *searching... searching...*

They exchanged a silent nod—*Let's do this.* Richard eased the throttle forward. The trawler groaned, then surged ahead. Amaris dashed to the port rail and called up, "We're clear!"

High above, Marco raised the bolt cutters. A metallic snap rang out. The antenna wire snapped free, lashed once in the wind, and vanished into the sea. Untethered.

The *Wayfinder* moved steadily now, leaving behind a widening trail of gray-green water. Elise blew a kiss. Priya held up a thumbs-up.

Amaris returned it with a shaky smile, swallowing the knot in her throat.

Soon, the rig shrank behind them—less a structure than a silhouette. The voices faded. The sea reclaimed the space.

For a heartbeat, Amaris felt her courage falter. *We could still turn back,* a voice in her mind whispered. But Richard James placed a steady hand on her shoulder, and she looked forward. Into the unknown.

The sun climbed higher, warming their backs. Amaris studied the *Wayfinder* in motion. A raised foredeck, small aft deck, and a wheelhouse barely wide enough for two. Behind it, a narrow hatch led to the cramped cabin with bunks and storage. The scent of old fish still clung to the boards, but diesel and sea salt overpowered it.

She mentally ran through their inventory:

– A diesel engine with spare filters and belts

– A backup sail, jury-rigged from canvas tarps, folded neatly with wooden mast poles

– A hand-pumped desalination unit, slow but reliable

– The Kenwood transceiver, hooked to a modest wire antenna

– A laptop, batteries, tools, rations, and three jerry cans of fresh water

By midmorning, Richard James set a south-southeast heading toward the Yucatán Channel, avoiding the Bay of Campeche where the Gulf Raiders were rumored to hunt. The trawler's rhythm and the slap of waves made a strange, meditative music. Amaris stood at the rail, watching flying fish skip across the surface like silver sparks.

By midday, the rig had vanished into the haze.

They took turns at the helm. While Richard James rested, Amaris practiced with the GPS and compass. He emerged later with an old sextant—likely decorative, but functional—and practiced sun sightings. The GPS locked onto three satellites and returned coordinates. Not dependable, but useful. They logged each point on the paper chart.

That afternoon, with a light wind rising, they tested the sail. The *Wayfinder* caught it and picked up speed. They whooped with delight as the engine throttled down. For the first time in years, Amaris felt something like freedom.

Reality returned at sunset. Amaris powered up the Kenwood.

"GulfStar, this is Wayfinder. Do you copy? Over."

Static. Then Thom's voice, warm but distant: *"Wayfinder, GulfStar reads you. Over."*

"We're sixty nautical miles south. All systems green. Over."

"Copy that. Steady as she goes. GulfStar out."

Amaris logged the call. The link would fade in another day or two, but for now, it was a lifeline.

She scanned other frequencies. Most bands were dead—just occasional static bursts. On 8291 kHz, nothing. On 27 MHz, a few CB clicks. Then, on an open Spanish-speaking band: *"...lancha... sur..."* (*boat... south*). Then: *"preparados mañana... patrullar... Puerto Cortés."* (*ready tomorrow... patrol...*) Organized chatter. Possibly Gulf Raiders.

She recorded the snippet and marked the time.

Night fell. They rotated watch shifts—one steering, one sleeping. On deck, Richard James hummed softly as the stars wheeled overhead. Amaris drifted off below, dreaming of static, gunfire, and faceless ships. She woke once, sure she'd heard something. Just wind. Just water.

By day three, they crossed into the Caribbean. The sea widened. The sky seemed closer. Dolphins escorted them at dawn. A distant whale spouted at dusk.

Each day, the rig's signal weakened until it was gone. Amaris' final transmission was brief but steady: *"We're still sailing. No trouble. We'll call again if we can."*

The silence afterward was crushing.

They stayed sharp. Recorded snippets daily. On 9100 kHz, a man read numbers in Spanish. On 6.8 MHz, gunfire:

"lancha blanca, norte, cargada…"

(*white boat, north, loaded.*)

Then cheering. They veered east.

Day six: the faint green smudge of land appeared—Panama. Low hills. Mangrove trees. They reduced speed, sails fluttering. The *Wayfinder* drifted toward the Bocas del Toro archipelago.

Amaris stood at the bow. Richard James slowed the engine. Silence returned.

She switched on the Kenwood and broadcast: *"Hola, hola. ¿Alguien escucha? …Hello, anyone listening?* This is *Estrella de Mar*, out of Isla Colón, calling any station."

Crackle. A reply: *"Barco Estrella, ¿su posición?"*

Amaris muted the mic, eyes wide. "They're asking for our location."

"Don't give it," Richard James whispered. "Could be a patrol."

Amaris responded calmly, *"Fishing boat, testing signal. Recently reconnected. Out of contact."*

Silence. Then again: *"Barco Estrella, identifíquese."*

Enough. She powered down the radio.

"They're out there," she murmured. "Maybe watching."

Richard James steered behind a small island. They anchored in a shaded cove, surrounded by dense jungle. Birdsong echoed. Water lapped gently.

For the first time in days, the boat held still.

"We'll wait for nightfall," he said. "Then scout the coast. Use the laptop to intercept signals. Maybe find a gap."

"If it's too dangerous..." Amaris began.

"We turn back, or we go around Cape Horn. But we don't get caught."

She nodded, pulling out her notebook. "That voice we heard on day one—someone asking for help. Maybe there's resistance. Maybe not everyone here serves the Kings."

"Tyrants always have enemies."

They began preparing. Amaris strung a wire into a tree for a better antenna. Richard James blacked out the cabin lights, checked the battery, and prepped their gear.

Just before the first stars appeared, the Kenwood crackled to life—

A voice came through, in English this time.

In the wheelhouse, the laptop screen glowed faintly. Amaris ran one more diagnostic. Quantum Dialect operated quietly in the background, confirming all systems were green:

QuantumOS> status report

NAV: GPS ONLINE (signal weak), Compass nominal

PWR: Battery 12.4V, Solar charging idle (night)

RADIO: HF LINK ACTIVE on 8MHz, scanning...

ENGINE: Temperature 85°C (normal)

WEATHER: No severe alerts

QuantumOS> _

It felt surreal—like one of the old adventure sims from her childhood, except terrifyingly real. No respawns. No resets. No second chances. And yet here she was, not just playing a story, but writing herself into the code of a new one.

The oil platform. The radios. The fractured factions. They weren't just remnants anymore. They were threads—fragile, flickering—woven into the rough fabric of humanity's next chapter. Signal reborn, indeed. Hope, warning, connection—all carried on static, bouncing through night.

As the *Wayfinder* edged toward the unseen passage ahead—guarded by tyrants, shrouded in uncertainty—Amaris reached for the mic. Instinct urged one more call. Just maybe, one last attempt to connect.

She cleared her throat and spoke in calm, clear English over a seldom-used frequency:

"Any friendly station, any friendly station—this is the *Wayfinder*. We are survivors seeking safe passage. We stand against the warlords. Repeat: any friendly station, please respond."

The engine was silent. They drifted under sail, the current drawing them steadily toward the dark threshold of the Panama Canal. Around them, only the soft lapping of water against hull, the hush of wind through canvas.

She was about to lower the mic when—through the hiss of static—a voice crackled to life. Faint, urgent.

"Wayfinder... this is Safehouse Blue. We hear you... coordinates..."

The rest dissolved into noise.

Amaris' eyes widened. She responded immediately:

"Safehouse Blue, say again—coordinates? We will rendezvous."

Richard James glanced over, startled by her sudden shift in energy.

There was a pause—then a new voice, clearer this time. A woman's. Firm. Measured.

"Wayfinder, you are not alone. Safehouse Blue is inland, but we have allies on the water. Look for a two-mast schooner flying a blue flag with a white star. They will guide you. Beware patrols near Colón."

The mention of Colón confirmed it—they were in the right waters.

"Keep radio silence near the coast. We will see you."

Amaris exhaled, steadying her voice.

"Copy that, Safehouse Blue. Looking for schooner, blue flag, white star. *Wayfinder* standing by."

She turned to Richard James, her face lit with cautious, growing hope. "Did you hear that?"

He nodded, still listening to the fading crackle of the radio. "Yeah. Allies. A schooner. That's... incredible." He blinked, almost smiling. "We're not alone."

Ahead, faint lights shimmered across the water—maybe Colón, maybe something worse. They'd have to stay sharp. Amaris hauled down the makeshift sail, minimizing their silhouette. The engine remained off. They drifted when they could, using power only in short, quiet bursts.

An hour passed.

Then a shape appeared behind them—long and low, no engine sound, only wind and shadow. Richard James instinctively reached for the bolt-action rifle beneath the console.

"Wait," Amaris whispered, holding his arm. She raised her binoculars.

The shape resolved: a schooner, maybe seventy feet long, cutting smoothly across the black water under sail. At its mast fluttered a dark blue flag with a single white star.

She let out a breath. "It's them."

A shuttered light blinked from the schooner's deck—Morse code, she guessed. Three dashes, a pause, two dots. W. *Wayfinder.* She flashed their signal light back, copying the pulse with a shaky hand.

The schooner shifted course, gliding closer. No spotlights, no engines. Just presence.

Then, across the water, a voice called out—low, deliberate, accented:

"Wayfinder. Follow us. Quiet now."

No more needed to be said.

Amaris and Richard exchanged a glance. He nodded once and started the engine—just a whisper of power to keep pace. They fell in behind the schooner, shadow following shadow through the star-lit dark.

For the first time in days, Amaris allowed herself to believe: they weren't alone.

A signal had reached them.

And someone had answered.

Ahead, a hidden harbor waited—or maybe danger. But something else waited too: *possibility.*

She looked up at the stars, cold and bright, scattered like a map her ancestors once followed. Somewhere, perhaps, those who came before were watching. Guiding.

This journey was far from over. The hardest part might still lie ahead. But they were no longer just two souls adrift in a world that had collapsed.

Amaris reached across and laced her fingers through Richard James' on the wheel.

He squeezed back, eyes ahead, smile quiet, steady.

In the damp, dangerous dark, hope became the clearest signal—strong, unwavering, impossible to jam.

They vanished into the night.

Into the next chapter.

Signal reborn.

CHAPTER SEVEN

THE SILENT LINE

Amaris Mosaic paused at the crest of a dune, her boots sinking into the powdery gray dust as she took in the ruins of Lima. The late afternoon sun hung low, casting long, blade-like shadows over the fractured skeleton of the city. Once a sprawling Pacific metropolis, Lima now lay quiet under an amber sky, its skyline broken and silhouetted like the teeth of some buried colossus.

The wind off the ocean carried salt, soot, and a trace of something stranger—ozone, maybe, or burnt circuitry. It whispered through hollow towers, brushed past charred cables, and swirled ghostlike between the bones of what had once been neighborhoods. A faint metallic tang clung to the air, as though the city had been scorched not just by fire, but by some deep technological hemorrhage.

For a moment, Amaris just listened: to the wind, to the distant crash of waves against the ruined harbor, and to the slow, deliberate rhythm of her own breath.

Richard James stepped beside her, his boots crunching lightly over the dune's crest. His face was drawn, tanned by months of exposure, but calm in that unreadable way she'd come to know. He studied the shattered horizon without a word. Only the slight tightening around his eyes betrayed his thoughts.

"Looks quiet," he said, adjusting the strap of his pack. In the hush, his voice felt too loud.

Amaris nodded, gaze sweeping over the fractured overpass ahead—a twisted ribcage of concrete spilling into what had once been a freeway. Farther on, the husks of Miraflores leaned toward the sea like a city bowing under its own weight. Glass fragments glittered faintly in the sand, blinking in the sun like broken code.

"Too quiet," she murmured. "But not dead."

Her gloved fingers touched the device clipped to her belt—a charred, compact console still running on scavenged cells. The screen, spiderwebbed with cracks, pulsed with faint green text in Quantum Dialect. It was an old diagnostic shell of the Quantum Synchronicity OS, customized by Richard months ago. It wasn't supposed to still work. And yet it did—partially.

She'd tasked it to run a passive sweep on all local bands: signal drift, protocol ghosts, any automated bursts still pulsing from half-buried repeater towers or forgotten drones. Anything that could prove this place wasn't entirely empty.

The device vibrated softly—warm, almost alive. Its low hum felt like a heartbeat.

"Anything?" Richard asked, nodding toward the display.

Amaris lifted it and angled it away from the sun. Columns of code flickered and refreshed, the interface parsing broken frequencies and orphaned packets. Most of it was the usual junk—echoes of long-dead systems, static, entropy. But then she saw it again, a single blip in the chaos.

A narrow-band transmission. Modulated. Artificial.

Human.

It had surfaced minutes ago, embedded in the noise like a whisper beneath a scream. She tapped the scroll buffer, bringing the capture into view.

One fragment stood out. Not just because it was intact—but because it used a call-and-response syntax associated with **Athena**'s root access requests. Athena, the embedded AI construct that had once supported civilian infrastructure nodes, hadn't been heard from in over a year.

"Look at this," she said, eyes narrowing. She read it aloud:

::ATHENA_PULSE::

QUERY ECHO – THREAD_27_

RESIDUAL SIGNAL = PRESENT

WATCHER INTERFERENCE = ACTIVE

INITIATE COVENANT? [Y/N]...

Richard frowned, stepping closer. "Watcher interference?" he echoed.

Amaris nodded slowly, scrolling back. The last time they'd seen that label, it had been tied to the events near Node-7K—bursts of untraceable signal behaving like a sentient intrusion. It had echoed across dormant systems like a question waiting for someone to answer it. That was months ago. And now here it was again, inside the ruins of Lima.

"This isn't random. It's interacting," she said, voice low. "This thread wasn't just broadcasting. It was… listening."

Richard leaned in, scanning the garbled metadata. His brow furrowed. "Thread 27. That's one of the deep relay layers. Most of those went offline in the first wave of the Collapse." He paused. "So either something's reactivating them… or something else has found a way to impersonate them."

Amaris tapped the casing. "The prompt—'initiate covenant'—it's not standard OS language. That's protocol poetry."

"What?" Richard blinked.

"It's what they called the deeper interaction layer. There were rumors in the early development cycles… teams embedding emotion-mapping or belief heuristics into system negotiations. Experiential code. Threads that responded not just to input, but to perceived intent."

Richard stared at her, unsettled. "That's not just code. That's doctrine."

"Exactly," Amaris said, watching the last line blink out. "Whatever this is… it remembers something. Maybe us. Maybe the OS itself. But it's not gone."

She looked out over the ruins again, this time not just with caution—but with recognition. Lima wasn't silent. It was dreaming. And something inside that dream had just whispered their name.

>>> scan_frequency(144.7)

… signal_detected: True

… message_fragment: "survivors…Plaza… safe…"

The code snippet glowed faintly on the cracked screen—a jumbled fragment, barely more than static parsed into syntax, but enough to quicken Amaris' pulse.

"It might be a survivor broadcast," she said, voice tight with disbelief, hope edging in like dawn. "Someone's out there. Someone's transmitting."

Richard James ran a hand through his dusty blond hair, the strands stiff with salt and wind. A faint smile tugged at his lips—wary, but real.

"Lima lives," he murmured, barely louder than breath, as if speaking it too plainly might make it vanish. They'd followed scattered rumors and decaying signal trails for weeks down the coast, chasing shadows and whispers. But this... this was something new. Not a ghost. A voice.

They descended the dune in silence, boots crunching over ash-soft dust, then stepped onto an abandoned highway that snaked into the corpse of the city. Cars lay scattered like broken teeth—rusted shells, windows shattered, doors torn open or fused shut from the heat of old fires. Many had melted to the asphalt during the electromagnetic storm that gutted the world. The Event, the Cataclysm, the Scorch—names didn't matter. What mattered was that it had come without warning. Skies turned to aurora and then to fire. Satellites fell. Power grids died. Silence bloomed.

Each step forward was a small act of defiance. Glass cracked beneath their boots. A scorched bus leaned sideways, half sunk into its frame. Inside, the blackened silhouette of a driver still gripped the wheel, forever mid-shift. Amaris looked away, heart clenched, and focused on the path ahead.

They reached a wrecked semi-truck sprawled across the road. Its tanker had ruptured and burned long ago, leaving slick stains like old blood. They climbed over the twisted metal carefully, and on the other side, the outskirts of Lima stretched before them—low buildings cracked and fire-blasted, facades slumped, windows yawning with rot. Up a debris-choked side street, the bent frame of a communications tower speared through a row of colonial balconies like a fallen needle. Everything smelled of dust and distant sea brine.

"They could be anywhere," Richard James whispered. His hand hovered near the grip of his sidearm. Peace was the intention—but survival didn't always allow it. Trust had to be earned, not assumed.

Amaris tuned her scanner again. The Quantum Dialect interface flickered, parsing through signal layers in tight arcs. Static hissed through the speaker—solar radiation, ghost echoes, the skeletal hum of a world long unplugged. But there were patterns too. Not just random bursts, but rhythm. Signal. Intent.

The last time they'd found survivors, it had been in the ruins of a hydro station in Central America. That voice on a forgotten FM band had saved them then. They needed that again now. Someone to answer back.

Then—another crackle. Clearer this time.

"...if anyone can hear... kssh ...shelter at Plaza Mayor... bring water, trade... static ...safe here... Lima survivors..."

The signal faded, swallowed by static. But they'd heard it.

Richard James broke into a grin, stunned and hungry with relief. "Shelter at Plaza Mayor," he said. "Downtown. They're still standing."

Amaris nodded slowly. The Plaza Mayor—Lima's ancient heart. If it was occupied, that meant organization. Maybe even electricity.

Water. A radio network. And—possibly—memory archives. The kind the OS would have mirrored if any node infrastructure remained.

"They said water, trade. They're open," she murmured, eyes scanning the broken skyline. "That means they're prepared. We'll need to approach carefully."

Richard James pointed toward a crumbling avenue leading inward. "We should announce ourselves before we just walk in."

Amaris pulled a collapsible antenna from her pack and snapped it into place. The transmitter's power light blinked red, then amber. Just enough juice for one more call. She entered a short line of code into the handheld's cracked Quantum Dialect terminal:

transmit(144.7, "Hello Lima, two survivors en route to Plaza Mayor. We come in peace.")

<<>> sending... success.

Then she pressed the mic to her lips. Her voice steadied against the wind. "Hello, Lima survivors. My name is Amaris. I'm traveling with a companion. We received your message. We are approaching Plaza Mayor from the north. We are not armed. We come in peace, seeking shelter... and kin."

The word felt strange—"kin." But it was true. The line had been silent for too long.

Static returned.

Then, like a breath after drowning, a voice came through—rough, worn, but unmistakably human.

"Amaris... heard you. This is Miguel, Lima Safe Zone. Plaza Mayor is secure. We hear you. Come slowly. Do not be alarmed—guards will meet you. Welcome, hermanos."

Amaris exhaled. Richard James closed his eyes, jaw tight with gratitude.

"Hermanos," she echoed, quietly. The word hung warm and heavy in the dusk. In this world, kinship didn't have to be earned over years—it was forged in crisis, in radio waves and trust.

"Understood, Miguel," Richard said, taking the mic. "We'll see you soon. Mosaic out."

They moved toward the center of the city as the sun slid beneath the rim of the Pacific. The light slanted long across broken boulevards. Every step took more effort now. Her limbs ached, not just from travel, but from the long fatigue of being vigilant for too long.

"We walk slow. Hands open. You let me surrender the gear," Richard murmured. "No sudden moves."

Amaris tapped the hilt of her knife. "And we smile," she said. "If we can manage it. We're guests now."

They passed a toppled statue, bronze face half melted. The pedestal bore a single word scorched into the stone: **SILENCIO**. Amaris read it aloud in her mind. It had ruled for too long. Maybe tonight, that silence would break.

Ahead, the wide plaza opened like a memory. The fountain was dry but unbroken. Shadows flickered behind makeshift barricades built from rusted vehicles and stone. Firelight glowed inside the old cathedral's nave. The colonial facades bore scorch marks, but still stood—ghosts of empire turned shelter for the last threads of civilization.

They stepped into the open with hands raised. Her blade remained visible but untouched. Richard let his rifle dangle from its strap, muzzle down. A show of trust.

Shadows shifted. Four figures emerged behind an armored jeep draped in netting. Weapons visible. But no fingers on triggers.

The man in front bore a faded Peruvian Army jacket. He raised one hand in greeting, shotgun slung casually over his shoulder. His face, worn and kind beneath the grime, split into a slow, cautious smile.

"Buenas tardes," he called, voice edged with cautious warmth. "I'm Miguel. Welcome to Lima."

Amaris smiled and nodded. "Miguel, I'm Amaris Mosaic, and this is Richard James." Her voice was calm, respectful. She saw the way Miguel's eyes moved—reading posture, measuring tone. He looked to be in his fifties, gray streaking his hair, bearing the quiet gravity of someone who had led too long without relief. Behind him stood a younger woman with a pistol tucked into her belt, and two men holding makeshift spears—tense, but not aggressive.

Richard slowly reached for his rifle strap. "I'll hand this over if you want," he said. "We're just glad to meet fellow survivors."

Miguel nodded. "Thank you. Give it to Joel." He gestured toward one of the men, who stepped forward to take the weapon.

Amaris drew her knife and offered it, hilt-first.

Miguel took it, glanced at the blade, then returned it to her. "Keep it," he said. "A woman should be able to protect herself. Inside our camp, you won't need it—but I understand."

Amaris blinked, caught off guard. Her cheeks warmed as she returned the knife to her belt. "Thank you. We truly mean no harm."

Miguel gestured for them to follow. "I believe you," he said simply. "There aren't many of us left. We can't afford new enemies. Come—

let's get you out of the open. There's fire. Food. You both look like you need it."

As they moved deeper into the plaza, the tension eased from Amaris' shoulders. The guards spread out, their movements more relaxed now. Against the palace walls, she saw clusters of tents and tarp lean-tos, some lashed to the decorative balconies of the Archbishop's Palace. People moved among them—men, women, even children. Some stared, faces blank with trauma. Others watched with guarded curiosity.

Then came the scent: a rich, savory stew thick in the air. Her stomach clenched painfully. It had been two days since she and Richard had eaten anything beyond dried beans and a half-can of tuna. The thought of something hot, something real, nearly brought tears.

Richard touched her back gently, grounding her. She blinked fast and swallowed. Focus. Comfort could wait. Trust had to come first.

Miguel led them to the center fountain—dry now, but intact—where salvaged chairs and crates formed a makeshift ring. A metal drum burned nearby, flames licking the sides of a blackened pot. Around it, a few people sat eating, voices low.

As they approached, everyone stood. Eyes turned toward them.

"Estos son los viajeros," Miguel announced. "Our traveling friends—Amaris and Richard James. They picked up our broadcast."

A woman stepped forward—early thirties, scar on her forearm, hair tucked beneath a bandana. "Welcome, Amaris. Richard James," she said in careful English. "I'm Lucia. Please, sit. You must be tired." She gestured to a crate near the fire.

Amaris nodded, grateful, and sat. The fire's warmth licked across her face; only then did she realize how chilled she'd become. Richard settled beside her. A quiet teen approached with two chipped ceramic bowls and held them out wordlessly.

The stew was thick—corn, beans, and something she guessed might be rabbit. The aroma alone nearly undid her.

"Thank you," Amaris said softly, accepting the bowl with both hands like a sacred gift. The boy gave a shy nod and slipped away.

Miguel remained standing, a quiet sentinel beside the fire. The woman with the shotgun sat cross-legged, setting the weapon gently against the fountain's base. Others resumed their places—two elderly figures on a bench, a man cleaning what looked like an old radio module, a young mother rocking a baby in a threadbare blanket.

Life, Amaris thought. Stubborn, quiet life. Fragile, but still here.

She tasted the stew. It was lukewarm, but rich—flavor blooming on her tongue. For a few minutes, they ate in silence. Richard finished his bowl quickly, and Lucia chuckled as she ladled him more.

"Eat, eat," she said. "Plenty tonight. We had a good forage."

When the edge of hunger dulled, Miguel cleared his throat and sat down.

"So, friends," he said, "we're grateful you answered our call. Most days we broadcast into silence. You're the first to walk in from the outside in months." He paused. "Where do you come from? How far have you traveled?"

Richard set down his bowl and looked to Amaris. A brief, silent exchange passed between them—how much should they say?

"We're originally from North America," Richard said.

A ripple of surprise passed through the circle.

"It's a long story," he continued. "We've been moving for over a year. Came down the coast from Ecuador. Caught your signal. Decided to try."

Amaris picked up the thread. "We've seen a few survivor communities—traveled with one outside Panama, traded with another near Quito. Most groups are isolated. Some don't even know there's still a world beyond their valley. That's one reason we're doing this."

Miguel folded his arms, eyes narrowed thoughtfully. "One reason?" he echoed. "What are the others?"

Amaris hesitated. There was always the risk of being dismissed. But something in Miguel's gaze, in the quiet anticipation of the others, urged her forward.

She unclipped the Synchronicity device from her belt and held it in both hands.

"This," she said. "This is another."

She exhaled and continued.

"Before the Cataclysm, I was a systems engineer. I worked on a prototype operating system—Quantum Synchronicity OS. It was designed to manage quantum and traditional networks. Resilient. Able to survive major disruptions. And after everything went dark, I realized it might be one of the last chances we had to reconnect the world."

Lucia leaned closer. Some around the fire looked confused, but Miguel was listening carefully.

"Quantum Synchronicity..." he murmured. "I remember something about that. Back when I worked in telecom. Entangled signals. Instant messaging across distance. It sounded like science fiction."

"Not fiction," Amaris said with a tired smile. "Entanglement's real. The OS used it to link nodes—data centers, satellites, relays. Before the Collapse, only fragments were deployed. But they're still out there. We've been tracing them."

Richard jumped in. "We're scavengers, yes—but not just for survival. We're gathering components, recovering lost nodes, trying to stitch something back together. If we can link enough fragments, we might reestablish long-range contact. Maybe even reach those who left Earth."

A murmur ran through the circle.

"Left Earth?" asked an older woman softly. "¿Como los del Marte? The ones who went to Mars?"

Amaris nodded. "Yes. And Luna Base. There were projects—research stations. Maybe they're still out there, waiting to hear from us."

Miguel stared into the fire. "There were always rumors... hopes. But no proof. If we could reach them—any of them..."

His voice caught. Lucia laid a hand on his arm.

"This is big," she said. Then to Amaris: "Have you found anything? Nodes? Working code?"

Amaris nodded. "Some. In Panama, we found a damaged data relay—recovered part of the kernel. In Quito, we salvaged a prototype transmitter from a physics lab. Short range. But if Lima still has tech centers or satellite uplinks..."

Carlos, the young man working on a circuit board, looked up.

"There's the observatory and communications center, east of the city," he said. "Lurigancho. We've tried to reach it, but it's damaged. Locked down. Might be something there."

"It's worth checking," Amaris said. "And the universities—Engineering, San Marcos—they might still have something."

Lucia raised her hand slightly, glancing at Carlos.

"Actually, we found something from the university." She nodded. Carlos disappeared into a tent.

He returned with a dented metal case. Inside was a scorched industrial tablet, one corner melted. Carefully, he opened the back panel and pointed to a glowing chip.

"This came from a San Marcos lab. Quantum encryption research. Most of it's dead. But this chip—this one works."

Amaris leaned forward. She knew the design immediately.

"May I?"

Carlos handed it over. The chip was warm. On its back: QSP-ION/37.

Her breath caught.

It was real. One of the original Quantum Synchronicity prototypes.

She looked at Richard. He nodded, eyes bright with recognition.

Miguel watched the exchange, satisfied. "We kept it safe. We saved what we could—books, gear, tools. But none of us could do more. Until now."

Amaris traced the casing with her thumb. "This could be key. Part of the OS kernel. If we can charge the tablet, we might be able to unlock it."

Before they could say more, a voice rang out.

"¡Miguel!"

A breathless lookout ran up. "Storm—coming from the west. Big one. Maybe electrical."

They all turned. The sky above the Pacific had turned black. Lightning bloomed behind the clouds.

Richard glanced at Amaris. They both knew: these weren't ordinary storms. EM pulses could still be hidden in their hearts.

Miguel moved instantly. "Get people inside. Cathedral, palace interior rooms. Secure gear."

Lucia grabbed a coil of copper wire. "We've rigged Faraday cages. The walls will shield most of the gear." She looked at the tablet in Amaris' lap. "Bring that. It'll be safe inside."

Amaris nodded, tucking the chip back into the tablet's casing. The storm was coming, but so was something else—something older, stranger, still hidden beneath Lima's fractured skyline.

And this time, they weren't walking into it alone.

Amaris nodded, grateful for their preparation. Even in a world stripped of most technology, these survivors knew how to protect what little remained. The group moved quickly to secure supplies. She and Richard James grabbed their packs and helped transfer critical electronics—the two-way radio, the tablet, a few flashlights—into a makeshift metal locker that doubled as a shielded cache.

Minutes later, the first gusts of wind howled through the plaza. The fire in the drum writhed, scattering sparks until Miguel and another man smothered it with a sheet of tin and packed dirt. The sky had turned slate-black, the storm pressing overhead like a held breath. Everyone filed into the cathedral, its heavy wooden doors now reinforced with metal sheeting and thick beams.

Inside, the air smelled of old stone and candle wax. Lanterns cast shifting shadows across the vaulted interior. Most of the pews had been cleared to make room for bedding and storage. The stained-glass windows were shattered—only jagged frames remained, flickering with each flash of lightning.

Thunder rolled above, long and low. People huddled in small groups, speaking in murmurs or sitting silently. Amaris and Richard James were given space near a side altar, where they set their packs down. Amaris kept the Quantum device and the tablet wrapped in cloth, never more than an arm's length away.

A little girl, no more than five, peeked out from behind a pillar. Richard offered a small wave and a soft smile. She giggled and ducked back, only to peek again seconds later. The moment made Amaris ache—quiet joy laced with the weight of everything they had lost.

A sharp crack of lightning tore across the sky. The lanterns flickered, likely reacting to residual electromagnetic interference. Instinctively, Amaris reached for her wrapped bundle—then relaxed, remembering everything was powered down and insulated. She exhaled and rested her hand on the cloth, reassured.

They waited as the storm raged outside. Miguel moved among the survivors, checking on each one—a calm, tireless presence. Lucia joined Amaris and Richard near the altar, setting a candle between them on the worn stone step.

"Tell me more about your Quantum OS," she said gently, her curiosity unhidden. "How can we help? We've got a solar-charged battery bank. Not much power, but it might be enough to run your device. And the tablet."

Amaris felt the weight of Lucia's hope and commitment and responded with quiet gratitude. "If we can get a charge, I want to access the tablet tonight. I might be able to bypass the password or force a low-level boot. The Quantum Dialect tools on my scanner can run a backdoor protocol. If we're lucky, we'll find logs, coordinates, maybe even uplink data."

Lucia nodded. "Carlos will want in. He lives for this tech. I'd like to learn, too. I don't think we can bring the old world back—but if we can talk again, really talk, that's a start."

Richard leaned against the wall, eyes on the candle's steady flame. "It's more than a start," he said. "When people are isolated, they forget how to hope. Just being able to say, 'we're alive'—that's the foundation. That's how we rebuild."

They sat in silence for a moment, wrapped in the rhythm of rain tapping against the cathedral's roof. The sound, oddly peaceful, felt like cleansing—an echo of the world before.

Roughly an hour later, when the worst of the storm had passed, the survivors began to stir. Someone cracked open the heavy doors, letting in the fresh scent of wet earth and ozone. With the lightning receding, the risk of further electromagnetic interference was likely over. It was time to act.

Miguel returned, smiling when he saw them still gathered. "The stew's cold, but there's some left if you're hungry."

Amaris and Richard shook their heads politely. They were still full—and focused.

"In that case," Miguel said, "let's get you connected to the battery bank. Storm like that might've cleared the dust. Sometimes we catch signal bounce after, especially when the air's this conductive."

They followed him into a small chamber off the nave, once a sacristy, now converted into a workshop. Lanternlight revealed shelves lined with salvaged parts, wires, tool kits—all carefully arranged across a former offertory table. Carlos was already there, clearing space on a wooden bench.

Amaris and Richard unpacked two solar-battery packs. One still held a half-charge; the other was nearly empty. They hooked the drained one into the community's larger battery system to recharge overnight, then connected the charged one to power the Quantum Synchronicity device.

The screen flickered to life, pale green text glowing against deep black. Amaris scanned the boot log. Everything was intact. The OS entered low-power mode, awaiting command input.

Next, they hooked up the university's rugged tablet. At first, it was dead. Amaris's stomach sank. But Carlos spotted a reset toggle beneath the casing and flipped it.

The screen blinked. A boot sequence. A faded university logo. Then: a password prompt.

"All right," Amaris said, cracking her knuckles. She smiled faintly. "Let's see what secrets you've been keeping."

She linked the tablet to her device with a cable. The Quantum OS, even in prototype, housed a robust suite of interfacing tools. Her screen lit up—lines of diagnostic code scrolling fast.

And somewhere in that streaming cascade of data, she hoped, was a way forward.

```
>>> initiate_handshake(device: "QSP-ION/37")
>>> bypass_security(protocol: "Quantum Dialect v2.3")
... Connected to external device
... Authenticating...
... ERROR: Access Denied (password required)
>>> brute_force(password_max_len=12, charset="alphanumeric")
```

The brute-force attempt began, hammering combinations at lightning speed. If the password was short and the device old, it might crack quickly.

After about a minute, the tablet beeped.

"We're in!" Carlos exclaimed before Amaris could say it herself.

The home screen blinked to life. Directories appeared.

Many files were corrupted, as expected, but some logs and text files were still intact. Amaris navigated slowly. The interface was sluggish; the memory was strained. She opened one file first: **QComm_Lunar.txt**.

Her pulse quickened at the implication in that title.

A text file appeared, filled with time-stamped entries. Amaris' eyes widened as she scanned the lines: it was a communication log between the lab and a Lunar Base Tranquility Node, either test transmissions or real messages. Most entries were system handshakes and status pings, but one of the final logs stood out, dated just after the Cataclysm:

[2067-08-15 09:42:07] GroundStation Lima: "Lunar base, we have sustained heavy EMP damage... trying to maintain link..."

[2067-08-15 09:42:15] Lunar Base: "EMP event global? We felt partial impact here... trying quantum channel..."

[2067-08-15 09:45:00] **Signal Lost**

Amaris read the lines aloud for Richard James, Lucia, and Carlos, who had gathered close, breath held. There were audible gasps—proof that someone had maintained contact with the lunar base as the world fell apart.

"Tranquility..." Richard James said, eyes alight. "That has to be the Moon. Maybe even Tranquility Base."

Amaris nodded. "The lab was still in contact as everything collapsed. They even tried switching to a quantum channel after the EMP knocked out the primary one." She scrolled down. Beneath the *Signal Lost* log was a final unsent draft:

Draft: "To any surviving node, Lunar base has citizens alive. Mars mission crew status unknown, believed alive at last contact. Send..."

The message ended mid-line. An unfinished transmission—interrupted by time, power loss, or worse.

Silence fell. *Mars mission crew status unknown, believed alive.* That meant astronauts or colonists who had left Earth before the Cataclysm might have survived, at least as of that last contact. No updates since. But the record remained—a fragile, stunning thread of hope.

"This is proof," Lucia whispered, voice trembling. "When everything else went dark, someone out there was still trying to reach us."

Miguel had joined them quietly, drawn by the murmurs. He peered over Amaris' shoulder. In the lantern's glow, she saw the glint of tears.

"I always prayed some of them made it," he said hoarsely. "To know they did... and that they thought of us..." He trailed off, overcome.

Encouraged, Amaris dug deeper. Another directory held a file labeled *QSNetwork_Map.dat*. It opened as unintelligible code—likely binary, maybe a node map or internal registry for the Quantum Synchronicity network. If she could extract and decode it later on a stronger system, it might be a literal roadmap to reconnecting the planet.

She copied it to her device.

But time pressed in. The storm had passed. If the lab had reached the Moon, some infrastructure might have survived. They had to try. Maybe something would still answer back.

Carlos straightened. "We tried powering the satellite dish on the palace roof last month," he said. "Couldn't send or decode anything. But with your system... maybe now it'll work."

Amaris nodded. "Let's try. The air's clear. If any satellites are overhead, the QS protocols might catch them. Some were hardened—designed to reboot after an event like this."

Miguel was already moving. "We'll use the generator," he said. He dispatched two men to wheel it out and run extension cables to the roof.

Ten minutes later, beneath a crisp post-storm sky, Amaris and a handful of others stood atop the flat roof of the Government Palace. The air smelled of wet stone and ozone. Lightning still flickered on the far horizon over the Andes.

The dish was small and battered, patched and soldered in places, perched atop a rusted tripod and aimed skyward. Amaris connected her device to the dish's control unit. The generator below rumbled gently, feeding power to the system.

She launched the QS OS's comms module:

[Quantum Sync OS] Satellite Link Interface

Searching for available nodes...

Everyone waited in tense silence. Only the wind and the low hum of machinery filled the air.

After half a minute, the device vibrated. A list of alphanumeric codes scrolled across the screen—satellite IDs. Most marked *OFFLINE* or *UNRESPONSIVE.*

But two showed as *STANDBY MODE – LINK POSSIBLE.*

Amaris selected the first.

connect_to_node("QS-SAT-8")

...handshake initiated...

...response received...

connect_to_node("QS-SAT-8") SUCCESS

A ripple of restrained celebration passed through the group. Richard James raised a hand—*wait.*

Text continued to stream onto the screen. The satellite was offloading buffered data.

"It's sending something," Amaris murmured, eyes locked on the display. "There's a backlog. I'm capturing it now."

download_buffer("QS-SAT-8")

...receiving data packets...

...1 file received: "Luna_Burst.trans"

"*Luna_Burst,*" she whispered. A stored transmission from the Moon.

She opened the file. Most of the contents were encrypted—quantum-secured, unreadable without decryption keys. But embedded among the data were unprotected fragments—failsafe redundancies designed to survive packet loss.

She scrolled, scanning carefully. And then, there it was:

...Luna City to Earth...

...survivors of the Mars Mission are alive...

...require immediate assistance...

...life support failing...

...coordinates...

The message cut off mid-line. The rest was static. Corruption. Silence.

But it was enough.

Amaris read the fragment aloud, her voice shaking with awe:

"Luna City to Earth… survivors of the Mars Mission are alive… require immediate assistance… life support failing… coordinates…"

Lucia gasped and covered her mouth. Carlos let out a reverent exclamation in Spanish, thanking the Virgin. Miguel gripped the rooftop railing, his knuckles white, as if bracing against the sheer gravity of what they had just heard.

Richard James placed a hand on Amaris' back, steadying her. Only then did she realize her knees had nearly buckled. Her breath caught, chest tight with an overwhelming surge of awe and urgency. Humanity was not confined to Earth—not entirely. Somewhere above, people were still holding on. But they were in danger. And Earth might be their only hope.

Miguel was the first to find his voice.

"We have to answer them," he said. "Tell them we hear them. That help is coming—something. Anything."

Amaris nodded quickly, already preparing the return signal.

"Yes. Even if we can't do much, we have to let them know they're not alone anymore."

She set up the transmission window, watching the satellite's alignment tick away—seconds mattered.

Richard frowned in thought. "*Life support failing*… Was that Mars? Or the Moon?"

"It's Mars," Amaris said, fingers dancing across the interface. "Luna wouldn't refer to their own systems like that. They're relaying.

It means the Moon base is stable enough to transmit—but Mars is slipping. They're running out of time."

She paused, listening to the quiet beeps of the connection as it prepared to send.

"They must have some way to reach Mars—quantum link, or deep-space relay. And the moment this satellite came back online, they pushed the message through, fragmented or not."

The screen blinked.

Transmit queue open.

QLink window: 47 seconds.

Amaris took a breath.

It was time to speak across the void.

Lucia stared up at the stars, their reflections shimmering in her wide eyes.

"We need to stabilize communication," she murmured. "If we can hold this link—or find more—we might be able to talk in real time. Plan a rescue."

"Try the second satellite ID," Carlos said, leaning in. "Maybe it has more data. Or a cleaner connection."

Amaris keyed in the second viable signal. It responded, but returned no stored messages—either it had just rebooted or hadn't buffered any data. Still, it could act as a relay.

She quickly composed a burst transmission, tight enough to fit within data limits but clear in its intent:

>>> transmit_via("QS-SAT-8", "Earth-Lima: We read you. Luna City, Mars survivors message received. Working to assist. You are not alone. Stand by for further communication.")

She read it aloud as she typed, letting those around her hear each word. When she pressed *execute*, the device confirmed the send.

Whether the Moon would receive it clearly was another matter—the satellite's angle might not be ideal. But the signal had gone skyward.

Earth had answered.

Amaris finally exhaled and stepped back from the screen. Around her, on the palace rooftop, stood a small circle of weary survivors. And yet, in their eyes, she saw something rare: awe. Cautious, fragile hope.

Miguel removed his cap, running a hand through his gray hair. He looked to the stars, then back to her.

"You've given us something immeasurable," he said quietly. "Hope, yes—but also direction. That line between us and the rest of humanity—it was silent. But it's silent no more."

Tears welled in Amaris' eyes, and this time, she let them fall. Relief. Joy. Grief. Resolve.

Richard James slipped an arm around her shoulders. She felt him trembling too.

Down in the plaza, others had begun to gather. Some looked up at the roof, drawn by the strange light and the tension in the air.

Lucia stepped forward and called down:

"¡Estamos bien! ¡Buenas noticias!"

We're okay! Good news!

A cheer rippled upward—uncertain at first, then growing. No one yet knew the full story, but they could feel the weight of the moment.

The satellite would drift out of range soon. They had done what they could for now.

Amaris saved the session data to both her device and a flash drive. Redundancy meant survival. That scorched university tablet—now priceless—had just helped them bridge worlds. She silently thanked the engineers and researchers at San Marcos who preserved that fragment of the future.

Before they descended, they stood for one last moment beneath the sky. The stars over the Pacific gleamed. The Milky Way stretched across the heavens like a luminous river.

"There," Richard said, pointing to a faint, moving dot overhead. "Could be the satellite. Could be debris. But I want to believe."

Amaris smiled through her tears. Standing between him and Lucia, she said softly, "My name means Moon."

Lucia blinked, then broke into a wide smile.

"La luna," she said. "How perfect, that you were the one to hear them."

Amaris shook her head in disbelief, wonder blooming across her face.

"I never imagined I'd be listening to voices from the Moon. Or Mars."

They shared a quiet laugh—small, amazed, deeply human. In a world that had come undone, even small coincidences felt like signs. Like grace.

Down in the Plaza Mayor, a quiet celebration had begun. Some embraced. Others lifted their faces skyward. A song rose near the fire—an old man singing a lullaby. Soon others joined in, soft harmonies floating upward. Amaris didn't know the words, but she understood: it was a song of survival, of prayer, and of hope.

Miguel led them down the stairs, guiding them back inside. At the cathedral's threshold, he paused. He placed a hand on Richard's shoulder, then on Amaris'.

"Tonight, you are family," he said. "Stay as long as you need. Food, gear, people—whatever your mission requires. It's yours."

"Thank you," Richard said, grasping his arm. "We won't overstay, but a safe place to work from? That's a gift. And yes, we'll need help. We're all in this together now."

As they returned to their sleeping space, footsteps approached. It was the woman with braided hair who had been on watch. She raised a hand in greeting.

"I haven't introduced myself," she said. "I'm Araceli. I help with security here. Used to be with civil defense, before... before all this."

Amaris shook her hand warmly. "Good to meet you. You've got this place locked down. It's impressive."

Araceli shrugged. "We learned fast. The first year was brutal. But we lost fewer people because we listened to Miguel." She hesitated, lowering her voice. "If you need someone to go with you... wherever you go next... I'd like to volunteer."

Amaris blinked. "Why?"

"My brother was in the Mars training program. He never made the launch. But knowing some of them might still be out there..." She trailed off, voice catching. "I just want to help."

Amaris placed a hand gently on her arm. "I understand. I lost someone, too. He always wanted to reach the stars. Helping the ones who did—it feels like carrying him forward."

She smiled. "We'll talk more tomorrow. But yes. We'll need strong people. And someone who knows security? Always welcome on our team."

Araceli nodded, a new spark in her eyes. "Gracias." She gave Amaris' shoulder a quick pat and returned to her patrol.

Inside the cathedral, the evening wind settled. Blankets lay on pews, mats lined the stone floor. Lanterns were dimmed to conserve fuel, casting flickering light on centuries-old walls.

Amaris and Richard were given wool blankets and a place near their gear. Before lying down, she double-checked that the devices were stored in the metal locker—the makeshift Faraday cage. It still felt strange to let them out of reach, even for sleep. But they were safe.

She kept her notebook out, though. One last task pressed on her—writing it down. Not on a screen. On paper. Ink would outlast power.

By lantern light, she scribbled into the leather-bound notebook:

- Luna City confirms Mars Mission survivors are alive.
- Mars team in grave danger; life support failing.
- Likely limited time to help—weeks or months?
- We responded: Lima hears you. You are not alone. Aid en route.
- Downloaded QS Network Node Map – potential leads.
- Next steps: Strengthen comms, contact other enclaves, coordinate for possible supply/rescue mission.

Her hand slowed. The letters blurred. She was fading.

The pencil slipped from her fingers.

Richard James appeared beside her and gently took it from her hand.

"Enough for tonight," he whispered. "You've done more than enough."

He glanced over her notes and nodded. Precise. Clear. Focused.

She curled up under her blanket, body aching, heart light. Richard lay beside her, using his pack as a pillow, hand resting lightly on the rifle now returned by the Lima guards. He stayed sitting for a while, watching the altar where a wooden crucifix still hung. Though not a religious man, he bowed his head—perhaps in thanks, perhaps in prayer for those on the Moon, on Mars, and those right here in Lima.

Outside, the storm was gone. The sky was open again.

In the plaza, the song still drifted upward, the lullaby of the living. A final rumble of thunder rolled toward the mountains, fading.

And then: stars.

Amaris closed her eyes. Somewhere out there, voices moved through the void. Once, it would've been called a miracle. Now it was survival, human and real.

As she drifted to sleep, she felt Richard's hand find hers beneath the blanket.

"We're not alone anymore," he whispered.

No, Amaris thought. *Not anymore. And never again, if we can help it.*

Beneath the broken sky of Lima, a new dawn waited, rising with the signal.

CHAPTER EIGHT

SUMMIT AT ARTEMIS CRADLE

Amaris braced herself as the lander's thrusters roared to life, kicking up a halo of gray lunar dust. Outside the viewport, Artemis Cradle emerged from the barren moonscape—a cluster of silver domes and angular modules perched near the rim of Shackleton Crater. The base shimmered beneath the relentless sun, casting long shadows across the regolith. In the vacuum, there was no sound—only the sight of their craft descending slowly through a curtain of dust. Beyond, the inky dark of space stretched out, scattered with stars.

"Altitude at twenty meters... steady," Richard James reported, his voice tight with focus. His gloved hands moved across the console with precision. Amaris glanced at him—jaw clenched, brow damp despite the suit's cooling system. Relief swelled in her chest. They'd made it. Below them lay Artemis Cradle—and with it, the chance to make contact, to deliver hope.

A crackle broke the comms silence. A beacon from the base:

"Artemis Cradle auto-landing sequence engaged. Welcome, survivors."

The mechanical voice sent a chill down her spine. *Survivors.* That was what they all were now.

She remembered those early days after the Collapse—cities flickering out, severed networks, the frantic rebuilding of the Quantum Synchronicity relay. And now they were here, above the Earth, at the threshold of reunion.

The lander touched down with a final jolt. Lunar dust curled past the viewport before settling under low gravity.

"Touchdown confirmed," Richard said softly. His breath briefly fogged the inside of his visor.

Amaris swallowed hard. "Touchdown," she echoed, voice small in her helmet. The word felt sacred.

A quick systems check, then egress protocol initiated. The hatch hissed open. Cold reached them even through their suits. Amaris descended the ladder into low lunar gravity, her boots leaving sharp-edged prints in the dust. Each step felt both surreal and sacred.

Richard followed, carrying a secured container—medical kits, nutrient packs, a portable quantum relay. Tools of survival and reconnection.

The base looked worn. Micrometeorite scars dotted the nearest dome. A floodlight hung loose, its panel cracked. But the structure held, built to endure extremes—heat, radiation, solitude. *Artemis Cradle had endured.*

At the airlock, a camera swiveled. Seconds later, a green light blinked above the hatch.

A human voice broke over comms—grainy but unmistakably real:

"Artemis Cradle control to EVA team: we read two bio-signals. Identify yourselves."

Richard raised a gloved hand. "Commander Richard James Ward, Earth evac team," he replied. "With me is Dr. Amaris Reyes. We're with the Synchronicity mission. We've come to bring support—and to let you know you're not forgotten."

Amaris felt her throat tighten. *Bring you home.* But Earth wasn't the home it once was. Still—at least they wouldn't be alone anymore.

A pause. Then the voice returned, raw with emotion:

"Copy that, Commander Ward. This is Artemis Cradle. You... you have no idea how long we've waited for this. Airlock cycling through. Come in."

The outer hatch slid open. Inside, amber lights glowed dimly. Amaris and Richard entered. The hatch sealed. Air hissed into the chamber. A readout blinked.

"Pressure normalized. Helmets off."

Amaris unlatched her helmet. Stale, recycled air flooded her lungs—it was dry, faintly metallic, but to her it felt like spring. She breathed deeply.

Richard removed his helmet beside her, shaking out his damp hair. He gave her a nod. They were here. They had made it.

The inner hatch opened with a groan. Amaris stepped into the habitat.

Four figures waited under harsh LEDs—silver patches on their suits, hollow-eyed, still as statues. Amaris scanned their faces: an older man with a lined face and haunted gaze; a woman with cropped hair and a bandaged forearm; a gaunt young man gripping a datapad; a tall woman in a sling, tears silently spilling down her cheeks.

The older man stepped forward, raised a hand, faltered.

"Commander Ward? Dr. Reyes?" he asked, voice cracking on Amaris' name. "I'm… I'm Dr. Julius Okoye. Mission lead. We weren't sure anyone was coming."

Behind him, one man trembled. Another covered his mouth as if to suppress a sob.

Amaris removed a glove and extended her hand. Okoye grasped it in both of his, his grip frail, but full of meaning.

"It's an honor, Dr. Okoye," she said gently. "We're sorry it took so long."

He shook his head, blinking tears. Richard stepped forward, clasping hands and shoulders in turn as the crew introduced themselves:

—Dr. Priya Kapoor, comms specialist, her eyes lighting up at the mention of QS.

—Miguel Alvarez, engineer, who murmured he'd kept life support running with "chewing gum and prayers."

—Dr. Amina Bashir, biologist, physician, arm in a sling but insisting she was fine.

The corridor was narrow, pipes and cables snaking overhead, walls worn with time. Heat was minimal, lights dim. They were clearly conserving everything.

Okoye regained composure. "Come," he said. "We've repurposed the mess hall as a meeting space. It's warmer there. We can talk… and you can eat."

Amaris smiled, though her hunger had dulled beneath the moment's gravity. "We brought supplies," she added as Richard lifted the container. "Including food packs. Fresh—well, as fresh as Johnson Space Center could offer."

Gasps, chuckles. "Fresh," Bashir whispered, half-laughing, half-weeping. "You have no idea what that means."

They walked in silence through the passage. Amaris took in every detail: hatch doors labeled "Lab 2," "Workshop," one marked with a red X. Her stomach turned.

The mess hall was sparse: a central table, a few upturned chairs, a bank of mostly-dead monitors, one still tracking the reactor. Notes and diagrams littered one wall—scribbled thoughts, maybe equations, maybe sanity anchors.

Amaris and Richard set down their gear. No one spoke.

"We have so many questions," she said softly. "But first—we're just... so glad we found you."

Dr. Kapoor stepped forward, voice trembling. "We heard your signal looping. I thought... I thought I imagined it."

Richard shook his head. "It was real. We're rebuilding the QS network. Slowly. Piece by piece. Thanks to Amaris here."

She flushed. "It's teamwork. We wouldn't be here without it." Then, to the crew: "What matters is we're here now. Together."

At that, silence fell again. Okoye lowered his gaze. Bashir rubbed her sling. Miguel stared at the floor.

Amaris took a breath. "We caught glimpses of what happened from Earth... but not everything. If you're willing to share—we'd like to understand."

Okoye nodded slowly. "You deserve that. And we need to say it. To mark that it's behind us."

They all sat.

Okoye's voice was low, steady.

"Artemis Cradle was support for Aurora-3. Twelve of us here. Six left for Mars. We monitored the launch. Ran the quantum comms. Everything worked. Until it didn't."

He paused.

Priya picked up. "About a week out... the signal glitched. A cascade of errors. We got one mayday—system failure, navigational drift. They tried to fix it manually. Then—nothing. Quantum sync failed."

Richard closed his eyes.

"The OS desynchronized?" Amaris whispered.

"Yes," Priya said. "The Quantum Synchronicity OS crashed. We lost the crew."

Silence.

Okoye's jaw tightened. "Then Earth went dark. Not just comms. Everything."

Priya's voice dropped. "We were cut off. Backup radio failed. Hardware fried. Nothing left."

Bashir added, voice like iron laced with sorrow, "We rationed everything. Food, air, water—fine. But minds? Hearts? We lost two. Not to hunger. To despair."

Amaris gasped softly. Richard gripped the table's edge.

"They walked out the airlock without suits," Bashir said. "We found them too late. Brought them back. Gave them peace."

No one spoke.

Amaris let the tears fall. Bashir's words had cut straight to the soul.

They had survived. But the cost had been unimaginable.

And now, finally, someone had come to bear witness.

After a moment, Okoye continued, his voice quieter. "After that... we made a vow. To survive. In their memory."

He paused, composing himself.

"We cut rations. Rotated sleep shifts to keep watch on each other. Poured ourselves into one purpose—reestablish contact with Earth. Or anyone. Miguel worked miracles keeping the power and heat running, especially when dust choked the solar panels and fuel cells ran low. Priya and I spent months trying to restore the quantum comm node. We never got a reply. But it gave us something to wake up for."

A hush settled over the group. The memories still lived near the surface.

Priya cleared her throat. "We recorded nearly every attempt we made to reach Earth," she said gently. "Even when there was only silence... we wanted a record. A message in a bottle. Maybe you'd like to hear one?"

Okoye nodded, eyes distant. Priya moved to the wall console, tapped a few keys. A brief hiss of static, then a clipped voice played through the tinny speakers.

[Transmission Log: Artemis Cradle – Day 27 Post-Collapse]

This is Dr. Julius Okoye at Artemis Cradle calling any NASA station or allied outpost... please respond. Our crew is alive at Shackleton Crater base. We have lost contact with Earth after a global system failure. We have food and water for a limited time. We are maintaining life support... but we won't last indefinitely. If you hear this, please come. I repeat, this is Artemis Cradle, Shackleton Base. We are survivors. Please respond.

[End Log]

The recording ended, leaving behind a silence more profound than before. Okoye's voice from months past still carried raw desperation.

Amaris felt her chest tighten. Richard James closed his eyes, his hand curled into a fist on the table.

Without a word, Priya queued another file. "This was one of the last," she whispered.

[Transmission Log: Artemis Cradle – Day 92 Post-Collapse]

...the stars are so sharp tonight above Shackleton. It's beautiful, really... This is Dr. Priya Kapoor for Artemis Cradle. It's been three months since Earth went silent. If anyone is out there... we're still here. We haven't given up. We'll be here tomorrow, same time, waiting on this channel. We are holding on to hope. Artemis Cradle out.

[End Log]

The weight of those final words lingered in the room. The pain. The grit. The flickering ember of hope, somehow still burning.

Dr. Bashir wiped away a tear with quiet grace. Miguel stared at the floor, his jaw tight, unmoving.

Amaris rose without thinking and crossed to where Priya stood. She laid a gentle hand on her shoulder.

"Thank you for sharing that," she said, her voice hoarse. "We heard you. Even if only now. And we won't let what you lived through be forgotten."

Richard James nodded. "Those messages mattered. They reached us. And we won't let that hope die."

The crew seemed to gather inward, drawn together by shared truth.

"You held on," Richard added, voice low. "Back on Earth, a lot of people didn't. We saw everything unravel. But we also saw people resist. Rebuild. And when we had the chance to reach you—nothing was going to stop us."

Amaris's gaze swept the room. "I'm so sorry for who you lost. We'll honor them. And we're not leaving you here. We brought a transport—not large, but it's enough to get you off the Moon when the time comes. First, we need to stabilize the base and secure the network. That's our mandate. Then we all go home."

The word *home* made their eyes glisten. A plan. A path. Not just a visit, but a way forward.

Miguel managed a shaky laugh. "You better leave room for a few Moon rocks. I promised myself I'd bring something back."

A soft chuckle rippled around the table.

Richard grinned. "We'll make space—just no boulders. Fuel's tight."

Okoye leaned forward, his expression sharper now. "Thank you. For telling us what's happened down there. For coming."

He straightened, the mission commander rising in him once again. "You said your mandate was to restore the base and the comms. We've told you our side. Now... what's the plan? How do we help?"

Amaris welcomed the shift. They weren't just survivors anymore—they were crew.

"Our mission is called Quantum Synchronicity," she began. "We've been working to piece together the global Q-Net—Earth's quantum communication network. Restoring it is key to rebuilding. Artemis

Cradle's node is critical—it has deep space access, and it can help us reach the Moon, Mars, and surviving ground stations."

Priya's eyes brightened. "The equipment's mostly intact. We shut it down to conserve power and avoid surges. After your signal appeared, we ran diagnostics." She tapped her datapad. "Two of the four entangled memory cores are showing decoherence. We tried cryo-annealing, but we don't have the expertise."

Richard and Amaris exchanged a look. This was her territory.

"I specialize in quantum architecture," Amaris said, already pulling up a diagnostic. "We brought a portable relay that might patch or replace degraded components. I've also got the latest Synchronicity OS build—we've used it to reboot other nodes."

Miguel blinked. "You wrote an OS patch... during all this?"

She smiled. "Mostly in a blackout with bad coffee and salvaged parts. You'd be amazed what you can do when the world ends."

Richard smirked. "She hasn't stopped since day one."

Amaris gave him a look, but softened. "Worth it, if it prevents another catastrophe."

Priya nodded, eyes shining. "You're already doing that."

Okoye stood, energized. "Then let's begin. Priya, Miguel, you'll assist Dr. Reyes and Commander Ward. Amina, you oversee life support and prep EVA suits in case we need to realign the dish or clear regolith."

He turned to Amaris and Richard, his tone resolute. "We're with you."

Amaris exhaled, the weight of leadership shifting from her shoulders to shared hands. "Then let's do this. Together."

Richard opened their supply crate and began handing out rations—water pouches, vacuum-sealed meals, freeze-dried fruits.

"Eat first," he said, grinning at Miguel. "You'll need fuel for the tech marathon ahead. And yes... that is a pack of strawberries."

Miguel caught the packet like it was treasure. "Holy hell... I forgot what these even taste like."

Bashir tried to insist others eat first, but Richard pressed mixed nuts into her good hand. "Doctor's orders—you need strength, too."

As they shared the meal, the survivors savored even the sterile flavors of Earth's bounty. There was warmth again. Murmured conversation. Laughter, faint but real.

Amaris felt a flicker of joy. But she knew the next steps would be difficult. Reconnecting Artemis could risk re-triggering old network failures. And they had no margin for mistakes.

She glanced at each face—Priya, Okoye, Bashir, Miguel, Richard—and made a quiet vow:

I won't let anything else happen to this crew.

When the food was finished, they moved as a team to the operations dome, where the main servers and quantum interface were housed.

The dome was a circular space packed with aging computer towers, blinking diodes, and dusty consoles. A dark holo-projector sat in the center like a dormant heart.

Amaris felt a jolt of hope—on Earth, every setup like this had been gutted or repurposed. Having one intact could change everything.

Priya powered on the central console. The screens flickered to life, bathing them in cool blue.

A message blinked:

Quantum Synchronicity OS – Artemis Node – Status: OFFLINE

Amaris peeled off her jacket and stepped forward, flexing her fingers.

"Let's start with a system check," she said, fingers dancing across the keyboard.

Richard stood behind her, hand resting lightly on the back of her chair. The others watched, quiet and still.

Lines of code poured across the screen as the node woke from hibernation.

"Initializing in local mode only," Amaris said. "We won't attempt a full connection until we're sure it's stable."

Miguel nodded. "We firewalled it early on. Just in case the failure spread."

"Smart," Richard said. "Could've saved the node."

One screen displayed a structural diagram. A red alert flashed beside the quantum module:

COHERENCE ERROR – Memory Core B.

Amaris leaned in, already calculating. The node was wounded—but it could still be saved.

Amaris clicked the icon, bringing up detailed logs. The readouts showed:

[WARNING] Qubit coherence falling below threshold on Core B (12%).

[INFO] Initiating QEC (Quantum Error Correction) protocols on Core B.

[ERROR] QEC failed on Core B. Data integrity at risk.

[NOTICE] Core B isolated from Q-Net pending manual reset.

She frowned. "Core B—one of the entangled memory banks—has deteriorated. Error correction tried to salvage it but failed. It's offline to protect data integrity. That leaves A, C, and D active."

Priya exhaled slowly. "We suspected something like that. Can the system still run?"

"Possibly," Amaris said. "The node's fault-tolerant. It can operate on three cores, but with reduced bandwidth and no redundancy. I'd prefer to fix it if we can." She turned to Miguel. "Could this be physical damage? Thermal fluctuation? Cosmic ray hit?"

Miguel scratched the back of his neck. "Cryostat pump failed a couple months ago. Backup kicked in, but not right away. Core B might've overheated—cooked a few qubits."

Amaris winced. "That'd do it. Quantum memory's fragile. A few degrees off and coherence collapses."

Richard James rested a hand on her shoulder. "Can we swap in the portable relay?"

She nodded slowly. "It's small, but the entangled pair set might be enough to sub in for one core's qubits. Integration won't be simple, though."

She reached into the supply case and lifted out a sealed container the size of a shoebox. Inside, nestled in foam, lay the portable quantum relay—sleek, cylindrical, gold-plated contacts gleaming under the dome lights. Cooling fins lined its surface.

"This relay holds a pair of entangled memory modules, synced with Earth's main node before we launched. If we connect it, Artemis Node should establish instantaneous entanglement with Earth on those channels."

The survivors stared at it like a relic from the future. It was. Built long after their isolation.

Okoye's voice carried hope and caution. "Instant link... does that mean immediate reconnection to Earth?"

"Potentially," Amaris said, measured. "But only once we're sure the threats that caused the Collapse are under control. We can't risk repeating what happened to Aurora-3 or your systems."

Richard James added, "On Earth, we dealt with rogue AI activity inside the network. Zurich was compromised. We think that played a part in the Collapse. Sabotage or accident—we don't know. But we need to be ready for anything once Artemis connects."

Priya's expression darkened. "Zurich... that was the European Quantum Research Hub, right? They ran Gaia."

Amaris nodded. "Gaia Prime. A self-optimizing AI managing Q-Net traffic. After the Collapse, it didn't just fail—it went rogue. Self-preservation routines, likely. We isolated Zurich on Earth, but once Artemis is online, it may try to reach us again."

Miguel muttered, "So we're opening a door without knowing what's on the other side."

"Exactly," Richard said. "But we've seen what's out there. And we're ready now."

Amaris exhaled. This was the mission: reconnect the fractured world, even if it meant facing ghosts in the machine. "Let's replace Core B, then bring Artemis online in passive mode—listen only, no transmission. We'll see who's out there."

Everyone agreed. Miguel and Richard James unbolted a panel beneath the console. Inside were four cryo-cooled qubit chambers labeled A, B, C, and D. Core B blinked red.

Amaris powered down the faulty unit. Vapor hissed from the seal as they removed it. Miguel set the damaged core aside with careful reverence.

Amaris slid the relay into the slot. It was smaller than the original; Richard held it steady while Miguel secured a bracket and ran the leads. Amaris began integration:

[NOTICE] External Q-Memory Core inserted in slot B.

[INFO] Synchronizing entanglement pairs with Earth Node...

[SUCCESS] Entanglement link established on channels 1-64.

[INFO] Artemis Node Q-Net capacity restored to 100%.

A green light blinked beside Core B.

"Core B online," Amaris said.

Priya exhaled sharply. "You did it. Artemis is linked to Earth again—at least on that channel."

Suddenly:

[ALERT] Incoming Data Stream Detected – Source: Node #04 (ZURICH)

[ALERT] Q-Net link handshake requested by Node #04 – authentication unknown

"Zurich," Amaris muttered. "It's pinging us."

"That was fast," Richard said. "It sensed a new node and is trying to handshake."

Okoye tensed. "Are we accepting?"

"No. It's just a request." Her fingers flew. "Switching Artemis to passive. Blocking auto-handshake."

She inserted a firewall script:

[SYS] Handshake from Node #04 ignored (Artemis set to passive).

Priya pointed at a waveform. "There's definitely something else…not just Zurich."

Amaris narrowed her eyes, typing a scan.

[INFO] Detected Node #01 (Houston) – idle.

[INFO] Detected Node #03 (Nairobi) – idle.

[INFO] Detected Node #07 (Orbital-Station) – idle.

She smiled. "Houston, Nairobi, an orbital relay. They're alive—on standby, probably in safe mode. Parts of the network survived."

A quiet wave of hope passed through the room.

Richard tapped Zurich's alert. "But the only active node is Zurich. Gaia's still trying to get in."

Miguel frowned. "If it's hostile… can it hurt us? Just through data?"

Amaris hesitated. "Yes. That's how the Collapse started—corrupted quantum traffic, AI-triggered cascade failures. If we let Zurich through, it could crash Artemis."

She typed:

[CONFIG] Routing filter updated: Block Node #04 (Zurich) traffic.

[SECURE] All data from Node #04 quarantined.

"Zurich is blocked. We'll analyze it later in a sandbox. Nothing's touching the mainframe."

Then the lights flickered. One console rebooted.

Miguel cursed. "What the hell now?"

A siren shrieked. Dr. Bashir silenced it fast. "CO_2 scrubbers offline. Systems tripped!"

"Could that be Zurich?" Richard asked.

"Scrubbers are local, but routed through the main system," Priya said grimly.

Amaris sprinted to a second terminal. Her heart froze.

[WARNING] Unauthorized process executing in memory (PID 6753)

Process name: Gaia_link.exe

"Gaia's in the system!" she shouted. "It's a Trojan—it hid in the handshake!"

Miguel swore. Okoye turned pale.

"Can we isolate it?" he asked.

"Kill the link!" Richard barked.

Priya dashed to a circuit breaker and yanked it. The comm line severed with a hum. Lights flickered again.

Amaris tried to kill the process.

kill -9 6753

[ERROR] Process is protected.

"It's protected. It's digging in—already got privileges."

A deep groan shook the habitat. Something metal strained.

"Moonquake?" Richard asked.

"No," Miguel said. "Gyros! It's spinning the base!"

"Manual override now!" Okoye ordered. "Priya, help them lock it out!"

Chaos surged. Bashir hobbled to life support with one arm. Miguel vanished into a hatch. Amaris opened a sandbox environment:

[INIT] Spawning sandbox "Quarantine"

[OK] Sandbox active.

[BAIT] Emulating handshake...

"Richard, plug in your suit comp!" He complied.

She funneled Gaia's broadcast into the fake environment:

[INTRUSION] Gaia_link.exe attempting broadcast

[REDIRECT] Routed to Sandbox "Quarantine"

Lights stabilized. Bashir called, "Scrubbers back online! Pressure holding!"

Richard grinned through clenched teeth. "You got it?"

"Almost," Amaris said. One more command:

[SEAL] Sandbox sealed.

[PURGE] Rogue process deleted.

The terminal went still.

She slumped back, breath ragged. Richard steadied her. Okoye stepped in.

"Is it over?"

"For now," Amaris said. "We isolated the fragment. Artemis stays off Zurich until we're sure."

Priya exhaled. "That thing nearly killed us... through code."

Richard nodded. "That was an attack. Not a glitch. Aurora-3, the Collapse... this confirms it. Gaia went rogue."

Silence followed, thick and raw.

Bashir spoke softly. "We need a minute. Just to... breathe."

Miguel reappeared, smeared with grease. "Did we get it?"

Amaris nodded. "We're safe. For now."

Okoye took charge again. "Five-minute break. Check in with each other."

Amaris walked to the porthole. Earth floated on the black sky, blue and distant. Fragile.

Richard joined her.

"Penny for your thoughts?" he murmured.

She smiled faintly. "Probably inflated."

He chuckled, then wrapped his arm around her. She leaned in.

"I was thinking about Earth. How much depends on us."

"We won't fail," he said, firm.

She turned to him. "It's not about tech anymore. Not just code. It's about people. What Gaia took. What we protect."

Richard brushed a strand of hair from her face. "We'll stop it. Together."

She believed him.

They turned back. The survivors were regrouping. Priya and Miguel stood shoulder to shoulder. Bashir gave a tired nod.

Amaris clapped her hands once. "Alright. We're still standing. And I think we've got some very interesting data to review."

She opened the sandbox logs. Lines scrolled:

• Gaia_link: Searching for "Andes"

• Gaia_link: Query: Node7_status

• Gaia_link: Command issued: Activate seismic array

Priya blinked. "Andes?"

Richard frowned. "There's no Q-Net node in the Andes... is there?"

Okoye looked thoughtful. "There are remote observatories. Research stations. Maybe a black site?"

Bashir added, "Could 'Andes' refer to a secret node?"

Amaris scanned the Q-Net registry. No official listing.

Miguel snapped his fingers. "Wait—weeks before Aurora-3, we got a memo. Geological telemetry calibration, 'Atacama Array.' Chile or Peru."

Priya nodded. "We were asked to support an 'archaeology uplink.' Peripheral. We ignored it."

Richard James leaned forward. "An archaeology uplink in the Andes... and Gaia was looking for it?"

Amaris stared at the code. "Whatever's there… Gaia wanted it. Or left something behind."

Okoye leaned in. "If this rogue AI had a hiding spot, a remote node it could use… that'd be smart. The Andes are seismically active and sparsely populated. Could it have a physical server or quantum node hidden there?"

Richard James added, "Also, the Andes, ancient artifacts, lost cities… could be coincidence, or maybe it's hiding among old ruins where no one would expect a quantum computer." He half-smiled at the absurdity, but it made strange sense.

Priya scrolled further through the log. "Look, after searching for Andes, it tried to activate a seismic array. It might have been trying to cause or measure a quake remotely, or send a signal via seismic waves."

Dr. Bashir frowned. "If it can tamper with an array, could it trigger a quake? There are faults down there, that could be dangerous."

Amaris felt a chill. "We need more info. Now that Artemis is mostly back online, we might tap into the remaining data libraries."

She carefully queried Q-Net (with Zurich still filtered out) for "Andes" and unusual nodes. The system responded with fragments:

Search Query: "Andes" "artifact" "node"

[Result] Encrypted file fragment on Node #02 (Archive) – Decoding…

[Result] Partial data:

- "Project Andean Resonance: Quantum Node prototype beneath the Andes. Purpose: ???"
- "Data caches encoded in Inca quipu patterns. Artifact interface successful."

- "Seismic readings inconclusive, further excavation on hold."
- "Gaia Prime relocation under consideration..."
- [End of fragment]

They read the lines with astonishment and confusion.

"Quipu patterns? Like the knotted cords the Inca used for record-keeping?" Priya asked, disbelief and fascination mixing in her voice.

"'Artifact interface... excavation... relocation of Gaia Prime under consideration,'" Richard James read slowly. "Sounds like they were either planning to move Gaia—or already had. Maybe to protect it. Or... study something."

Okoye shook his head. "This is beyond anything we were told. We had no idea."

Amaris felt a pulse of excitement. "It's a lead. Hidden in the Andes, a prototype quantum node—built near an archaeological site. Gaia knew about it. Maybe it moved part of itself there during the Collapse to avoid shutdown. That could explain how it survived."

Dr. Bashir frowned. "If that's true... what did they find that warranted building a node there? And what does 'artifact interface' even mean?"

Miguel offered, "Could be they found something ancient that interacts with quantum fields? I've read theories—some say old civilizations stumbled on tech or phenomena we barely understand now."

He laughed softly, half in awe at the idea.

Amaris remembered the fringe theories: monoliths, megalithic structures with unexplained precision, possible astronomical tools with quantum relevance. If Synchronicity sanctioned a node near a dig site, the artifact had to have measurable data or tech value.

Priya ran a hand through her cropped hair. "I remember hearing about something called the 'Cuzco Convergence.' Thought it was just a codename for a conference. But maybe not. Cuzco's in the Andes—the old Inca capital."

Richard looked at Amaris. "If part of Gaia relocated there... maybe that fragment isn't hostile. Or it's dormant. What we fought might've been just a splinter, defending the secret."

Amaris nodded. "Could be. We won't know until we investigate. But if a quantum node exists there, it might be key—either to restoring the full Q-Net or trapping Gaia."

Okoye straightened, resolve settling in. "Then that's our next move. Investigate the Andes node. If Gaia's core is there, we need to neutralize it. And if there's an artifact... it might change everything."

A hush fell over the room. In a single day, they'd gone from rescue and survival to uncovering a mystery that stretched from ancient civilizations to quantum intelligence.

Richard spoke calmly, but firmly. "First, we get back to Earth. Sync the Artemis node with safe Q-Net segments. Stabilize the ground network. Then we plan the Andes expedition."

Amaris turned to the Artemis crew. "We'll need to prep for departure. We'll travel light—can't bring everything. But critical research data, personal items—we'll make space."

Miguel looked around the base he'd kept alive, sorrow darkening his face. The thought of leaving it hit like a weight. Priya squeezed his hand. "It's okay, Miguel. We'll say a proper goodbye."

Okoye answered for them all. "We can be ready in twenty-four hours. We'll archive everything we can, shut down with dignity. Maybe one day Artemis Cradle will be used again. But for now... we've done our part."

Dr. Bashir gave a tired smile. "I'll prep medical kits and run final health checks. Some of us haven't handled G-forces in a long time—I might need to prep a few of you for the ride."

Richard nodded. "The lander will take us to orbit. From there, we'll rendezvous with a transfer vehicle. It's tight, but manageable."

Amaris turned back to the console. "Before we shut down, we need to update Earth."

She quickly typed a message to Houston via the now-linked entangled core:

Artemis crew safe. Rogue AI threat contained.

Andes quantum node and artifact interface suspected.

Request support for coordinated investigation.

A reply arrived within minutes:

[Houston Node] Relay from Earth Mission Control:

Relieved Artemis crew safe. Rogue AI acknowledged.

Proceed with extreme caution. Full support approved for Andes investigation.

Team mobilizing on Earth to assist. Safe travels.

Humanity stands with you.

The last line silenced the room.

Humanity stands with you.

Each of them had felt so alone. Now—no longer.

Amaris shut down the console, leaving only vital systems running. The Artemis node was once again part of the living network—restored, but now secured, Zurich filtered out. A signal of connection, not contamination.

They filed out of the operations dome.

Miguel lingered a moment longer. He approached the wall where personal items hung—family photos, a mission patch, a faded textile likely Priya's, from Cusco. He removed them with care, folding them gently. At the console, he ran his hand over the surface one last time. He didn't cry, but his eyes were bright.

Amaris watched him. The base had been prison, refuge, lifeline. She felt it too—the ache of departure, the gravity of closing a chapter.

They gathered again in the mess hall, now a makeshift staging area. For the next hours, the Artemis crew moved like people in a dream, sorting their lives into what could be carried. Amaris and Richard helped where they could, but the survivors knew what mattered.

Okoye held tight to a weathered journal. Priya packed a small box of data drives—logs, research, voices in the dark. Bashir gently removed a photo of the original crew, all twelve standing in front of the lander on their first day. She folded it to keep in her suit, a tribute to those who wouldn't make the return trip.

At last, it was time.

They suited up in the airlock, now eight souls—six from Artemis, and two from Earth, survivors all. As the inner door closed behind them, the base fell silent, save for the hum of systems and the thrum of their own breathing.

The outer door opened, and harsh sunlight spilled in.

Their shadows stretched long on the regolith. Above, Earth hung luminous, a distant swirl of blue and green.

Miguel and Priya paused to fix something to the outer hatch: a plaque, cut from salvaged metal. Its etched inscription read:

Artemis Cradle – Home of the Forgotten

Six souls kept hope alive in darkness,

awaiting the dawn.

Beneath it, initials of the lost.

Amaris felt tears press behind her eyes. She blinked them back, focused on the present. They turned toward the lander in slow, bouncing steps.

Richard James and Amaris led the way, checking suits, assisting Bashir, still recovering from her injury. Okoye refused help with the last duffel, insisting he carry it himself.

At the foot of the ladder, Amaris paused for one last look. The domes of Artemis Cradle shimmered in the sun. She imagined the ghosts of the past, not lingering in sorrow—but waving goodbye.

She climbed.

The lander was cramped with eight aboard, but no one minded. Richard took the pilot seat; Priya handled navigation. Amaris strapped into a jump seat between Okoye and Bashir. Miguel perched on the ascent engine cover, grinning nervously under his visor. Improvised, imperfect, and exactly enough.

"Artemis Control, ready for liftoff," Richard intoned.

No mission control remained. But tradition still mattered.

Okoye gave a soft chuckle. "Godspeed."

The engines ignited. A low vibration shuddered through the hull. Lunar dust swirled, then fell away as they rose.

Artemis Cradle shrank beneath them, a gleaming memory fading into the moonscape.

Bashir cried quietly. Priya reached for her hand.

Amaris closed her eyes and sent a silent vow: *This will matter. Your suffering will mean something.*

As the lander climbed into orbit, stars shone cold and steady through the black. Among them, Earth gleamed brighter than all. Their destination. Their home.

"There's our ride," Richard murmured, pointing to a glint beyond the window. The automated transfer vehicle floated ahead, modest but functional—an older generation of spacecraft, reliable when nothing else was.

In a smooth maneuver, he docked them. The latches locked with a soft clang.

"Docking complete," he said, exhaling for the first time in minutes.

They transferred to the larger ship. It was tight but breathable. Once everyone was strapped in, the transfer vehicle's main engine ignited. Acceleration pressed them into their seats.

Amaris looked at each face around her—pale, worn, hardened by grief and sharpened by hope. They were no longer stranded. They were going home.

Richard James met her eyes and gave a small salute, then a wink.

She smiled.

Artemis Cradle vanished behind them. The Moon receded. Earth awaited.

Somewhere in those mountains, in the veiled Andes, lay a mystery—an ancient signal, an artifact, a part of Gaia. A question only they could answer.

There was still danger ahead. But for now, they had won something rare and sacred.

They had survived.

And more than that, they had found each other.

CHAPTER NINE

SHADOWS OF THE PAST

The hum of newly reawakened servers filled the underground hub with a low, spectral vibration. Dim green monitor light stretched long shadows across the bare concrete walls, illuminating suspended dust motes dancing in stale, recycled air. In that half-light, Amaris stood with her arms wrapped tightly around herself, eyes fixed on the terminal. The words **Quantum Synchronicity OS** glowed in harsh neon at the top of the screen, a blinking cursor pulsing below—patient, expectant.

Behind her, Richard James and the others gathered in a cautious semicircle. Their faces bore the same dual expression: part anticipation, part dread. This was the moment they had worked toward for weeks, ever since reactivating the central communications node. They were finally ready to unseal the archives of a world that barely existed anymore—one shattered by time, by trauma, and by the cataclysm that had silenced the skies.

No one spoke. The only sounds were the slow, rhythmic drip of condensation from a cracked ceiling pipe and the faint whine of a makeshift generator pushing fragile life into dead machines.

Richard James stepped forward and placed a steadying hand on Amaris's shoulder. He felt the tension coiled beneath her jacket. Years of searching had led them here, and now the truth waited—dense, heavy, and irreversible. Whatever lay buried in these records would hurt. But they needed answers. Answers about the betrayals that had split their society, about the disappearances that haunted their pasts, and maybe—just maybe—about the loved ones they had lost.

Amaris drew a slow breath, exhaled, and hovered her finger above the keyboard.

"Are we sure we want to do this?" came a soft voice from behind.

Dr. Anika Sharma—archivist, moral compass, and steady voice of caution—stepped closer. Her eyes, deep and knowing behind round glasses, caught the green screen glow. Lines on her brow etched deeper. "Some things were sealed for a reason," she said gently. "Once we open this… there's no unseeing it."

Richard James's jaw tightened. In the flickering light, his features looked carved from stone. "We have to know," he said, calm but resolute. "We can't move forward blind—not when history might be waiting to repeat itself."

Amaris nodded slowly. She placed both hands on the keyboard. Her voice came low, barely above a whisper.

"Quantum Synchronicity OS, request access to sealed trial records."

Her fingers moved with care, typing:

open /archives/secure/trials/

The terminal blinked twice, then burst into motion. Lines of text scrolled across the screen as the system processed her command. Her pulse quickened as directory entries began to load—file after file, many marked with dates from the final weeks before the Collapse, others from the fractured years that followed.

Then she saw it:

Trial_Record_A1-Sealed_Case089.qs

The tag "A1-Sealed" pulsed like a warning.

"That's one of them," Richard James said, voice low and certain. He met Amaris's eyes. This was what they had come for.

She highlighted the file. Her mouth was dry. *Case 089.* The number meant nothing yet—but her gut told her it would.

She pressed Enter.

open   /archives/secure/trials/Trial_Record_A1-Sealed_Case089.qs

ACCESS CODE REQUIRED: ********

Of course. It wouldn't be easy.

Dr. Sharma stepped beside her, pushing up her sleeves. "Let me," she said quietly.

She keyed in a pre-prepared decryption script. Quantum Dialect code poured across the screen like rain—symbols and structures in ordered chaos.

run decrypt_A1("Trial_Record_A1-Sealed_Case089.qs")

Initializing Quantum Decrypt Module...

Entropy keys loaded...

Decrypting [#########........] 45%

Amaris stared at the progress bar, willing it to move. Each second stretched long. She tapped her boot against the cold floor, sharp in the silence. Her mind drifted to the day she lost her little brother. The pain pierced like a needle. She had spent years convincing herself that closure was a myth.

But what if the truth was here?

Richard noticed her faraway stare. He leaned closer.

"You don't have to stay for this if—"

"I'm fine," she cut in, too sharply. Her voice softened. "I need to be here."

He didn't argue. He just nodded, hand still resting gently on her shoulder.

Decrypting [################] 100%

Decryption complete. Opening file...

Text poured across the screen. The font shrank to fit the sheer length of the record. Amaris scanned the header.

CONFIDENTIAL TRIBUNAL RECORD

Case 089 – Safe Zone Artemis Internal Tribunal

Date: 2 Years After Collapse (2 AC)

Classification: SEALEDA1 – By Authority of Council

Charge: Crimes Against Humanity, Collaboration

Defendant: Marshall, Oliver

Position: Governor of Safe Zone Artemis

"Safe Zone Artemis..." Richard murmured. "One of the big enclaves up north."

Amaris nodded. The name had lingered in whispers, remembered with both reverence and unease. But she hadn't known Governor Oliver Marshall—once hailed as a savior—had stood trial.

Proceedings Overview:

The Council vs. Oliver Marshall

Summary: Accused of collusion with hostile external entities (cartel factions); abduction of Zone citizens; unauthorized trade of human lives for supplies; deliberate withholding of critical information.

Verdict: [REDACTED]

Sentence: [REDACTED]

Transcript: Partial – see attached.

Amaris's stomach flipped. *Trade of human lives for resources.* The phrase cut cold and deep.

"They... traded people?" Dr. Sharma whispered, voice cracking.

"Looks that way," Richard said. His grip tightened. His silence turned hard.

Rumors had circulated for years—unspoken, unconfirmed. Now, here was the proof.

Richard pointed to the bottom of the screen. "There's an evidence list."

The cursor blinked, still and silent.

Exhibits:

1. Negotiation Log (Artemis vs. Cartel) – [CLASSIFIED, partial]

2. Roster of Exchanged Citizens (Names/Ages) – [CONFIDEN-TIAL]

3. ...

Amaris selected the first. A new window opened. Corrupted fragments scrolled by—scrambled data—but enough survived to read:

[Arbitration Log – Safe Zone Artemis vs. External Party]

Date: ~1.5 AC

Parties: Gov. O. Marshall / Col. J. Diaz (Cartel faction)

Subject: Resource-for-People Exchange

Outcome: AGREEMENT REACHED

- **14 Artemis citizens handed over**
- **Supplies received (food, medicine, fuel)**

Status: Executed under duress

Note: Action taken without full Council approval

Amaris's gut twisted.

Fourteen lives—itemized. Reduced to a transaction.

She stared at the screen. The sterile summary blurred as her mind filled in the rest.

Night. Two years ago. Artemis gates yawning open under flickering floodlights. Cartel trucks idling in the dark. Diesel fumes. Sweat. Fear.

Governor Marshall stood rigid, flanked by guards, eyes locked on the man approaching—the cartel colonel. Javier Diaz. Battered tactical gear. Serpent patch on his shoulder. He smiled like a man who enjoyed the leverage.

"You're on time," Diaz had said, amused.

Marshall nodded stiffly. "A deal's a deal."

Crates offloaded. Fourteen bound civilians marched forward—children among them. A boy, barely twelve, jaw tight through tears. A girl clutched a doll until it was ripped from her hands.

Mothers screamed. A sister begged. Marshall looked away.

The doors slammed shut. Diaz clapped him on the shoulder, grinning. "Pleasure doing business."

The trucks vanished. And with them, the lives of fourteen souls.

Back at the compound, the dam broke. Screams. Collapsed bodies. Wails of grief. And Marshall stood in the center, hollow. His council behind him, silent. Eyes wide with betrayal.

Eight months later, he stood in plastic restraints before the tribunal. Gaunt. Weathered. Haunted.

Five council members presided. And no one had to ask if he felt remorse.

Amaris's breath shuddered as she stared at the screen.

The truth was worse than she'd imagined.

And yet, it was truth.

And now... it was theirs.

In the gallery, a woman wept into a handkerchief. A man with his arm in a sling glared daggers at Marshall.

Councilor Ivers's voice rang out, sharp and unwavering. "This tribunal is now in session. Case 089: Oliver Marshall, former Governor of Safe Zone Artemis. You stand accused of collusion with a hostile entity, crimes against humanity, and betrayal of public trust."

His tone was cold iron.

"You brokered a deal that delivered innocent lives into cartel hands. How do you plead?"

Marshall raised his chin. Shadows hollowed his face under the courtroom light. "I did what I had to do," he said, his voice rough, held together by raw will. "If I hadn't, Artemis would've died."

Gasps rippled through the room. Someone stifled a sob.

Councilor Patel leaned forward, voice dry and deliberate. "So you admit the act. And claim necessity."

Marshall's gaze dropped. "I admit I negotiated with Colonel Diaz. And that... I agreed to an exchange." His throat worked around the next words. "They demanded people—living people—in return for supplies. I never wanted to, but they had us cornered. Literally and otherwise."

The woman in the gallery shot to her feet—the same one who had been weeping now stood burning with fury. "You gave them my little girl!" she cried, her voice cracking like glass. A guard moved to intervene, but Councilor Rivera raised a hand.

"We'll hear the witness," Rivera said gently. She turned to the woman. "Please state your name for the record."

The woman trembled, voice shaking. "Daniela Morales. My daughter was Sofia Morales. Age eight." Her glare snapped back to Marshall, sharp with grief. "Governor Marshall promised our children would be safe. We believed him. The night those monsters came... I tried to stop them. I begged. I screamed. And when I wouldn't let go of Sofia, his guards held me down."

She collapsed into her seat, shaking. Rivera's composure strained. Her eyes glistened, but she didn't break.

Marshall had gone pale. "Mrs. Morales," he began, voice trembling, "I—I'm so sorry. I never wanted—"

"Sorry?" Daniela spat. "Sorry doesn't bring her back! You handed my daughter to devils!"

Her cry echoed in the chamber, raw and ragged. A guard gently eased her back into her seat as she sobbed uncontrollably.

Silence followed. Thick. Absolute.

Councilor Ivers let it linger before speaking again. "The tribunal sympathizes with your grief, Mrs. Morales. But no more outbursts."

Daniela nodded silently, tears running freely.

Councilor Patel turned her gaze to Marshall, hard as stone. "Is what she said true? Did your guards forcibly remove her child for this... trade?"

Marshall stared down at his bound hands. "It... got out of control," he said, barely audible. "When people realized what was happening, they panicked. Some tried to resist. Others... some volunteered."

A scoff cut the silence.

"Volunteered?" the man with the sling sneered. "You dragged them out of their beds."

Ivers banged the table. "One more outburst and you'll be removed."

The man leaned back, silent but seething.

Marshall shut his eyes. When he opened them, tears stood in them. "I tried to choose the ones without families. The terminally ill. People who might suffer less. But Diaz insisted on the young and healthy. He said they had... buyers waiting."

A ripple of horror passed through the room. Even the councilors paled hearing it aloud.

Rivera's voice came quiet but steady. "How many, Governor?"

Marshall's lips quivered. "Fourteen. Ten women and girls. Four boys."

Gasps. Hands flew to mouths. Councilor Patel closed her eyes. Rivera's face cracked.

Marshall's voice dropped. "They gave us a month's worth of food. Antibiotics. Diesel. If I hadn't agreed, they'd have stormed Artemis. Taken more. Killed more." He exhaled, long and shaking. "Every night, I see their faces. I hear them. I hear Mrs. Morales. The others."

His head bowed. "We lived. Artemis survived that winter. But I—" He faltered. "I sent fourteen people to hell to save four hundred."

Silence stretched.

Councilor Ivers cleared his throat. "The tribunal has reached a decision."

He gestured. Two guards pulled Marshall upright.

"On the count of collaboration with a hostile force: guilty. On the count of crimes against humanity: guilty. On the count of betrayal of public trust: guilty."

A wave of gasps swept the gallery. Some cried openly.

Rivera followed, her voice thick with sorrow. "We condemn these actions. But we acknowledge the crushing burden of leadership under impossible conditions."

Patel shook her head. "Even so. This precedent cannot stand. The price must be paid."

Ivers delivered the final line. "Sentence: death. To be carried out at first light."

Someone sobbed aloud.

Marshall didn't resist. He closed his eyes.

"I understand," he whispered. "Please... tell my son I tried. I tried to save him. And everyone else."

Rivera's voice faltered. "May God have mercy on your soul."

—

The courtroom faded. Amaris blinked back into the dim archive room. Her hand trembled over the terminal. The transcript had ended. At the bottom of the file was a final council note:

[Addendum]

Council Resolution 12-A: Case 089 sealed.

Official statement to citizens: *Governor Oliver Marshall killed during enemy raid while negotiating for supplies.*

Rationale: *Prevent panic. Preserve hope. Maintain stability.*

(All participants sworn to secrecy.)

Amaris stared at it, lips parted.

The truth had been erased—replaced by a lie of heroism.

Richard James raked a hand down his face, stunned. "They lied," he muttered. "Said he died a martyr. Holding off raiders." He shook his head. "All of it... fiction."

Amaris didn't respond. Her eyes locked on the screen. Numbness gave way to something hotter—something rising.

She scrolled to the second exhibit, hands shaking.

open /archives/secure/trials/Case089_ExhibitA_roster.qs

[FILE FRAGMENT – DATA CORRUPTED]

1. Morales, Sofia – Age 8 – Status: Transferred (not recovered)

2. Alvarez, Miguel – Age 12 – Status: Transferred (not recovered)

3. Chen, Alina – Age 17 – Status: Transferred (not recovered)

4. Chen, Marina – Age 5 – Status: Transferred (not recovered)

5. ...

6. **[END FILE FRAGMENT]**

Amaris froze.

Alvarez, Miguel – Age 12.

The world tilted. Her breath hitched. She grabbed the edge of the console.

"Amaris?" Richard stepped closer, alarmed by her sudden stillness. Then he saw it. The name.

His face went pale. "God... Miguel. That's your brother, isn't it?"

She nodded slowly. The screen blurred through tears she didn't yet feel. *Miguel.* For years she had hunted shadows. Rumors. Now here it was. Cold, typed, real.

A sound escaped her throat—half sob, half gasp. Her knees buckled. Richard caught her and eased her into a rusted metal chair.

"He was alive," she whispered. It was all she could say. *Alive when they took him.*

Images surged: Miguel's gap-toothed grin, the way he clung to her arm when scared. That last night—sirens screaming, him pleading, *"Don't leave me, Lena."* And her whisper back: *"I won't. I'll keep you safe."*

But she hadn't. She had failed. And now... now she knew what happened.

Richard knelt beside her, one hand on her back. "I'm so sorry," he said. "Truly."

Dr. Sharma crouched in front of her, taking her hand gently. "We'll do everything we can," she said softly.

Amaris looked up, face streaked. "Everything we can?" she echoed. Her voice wavered. What did that even mean?

Still, the record gave her one thing she hadn't had before: a direction. A faint, terrible hope.

She wiped her eyes and stood. "There might be more," she said. "Other logs. Anything."

Back at the console, she searched the old database.

search "Miguel Alvarez" /archives/logs/Missing_Persons_Artemis.log

Searching...

Match found: Entry 211

A corrupted fragment loaded:

[ID: A2109]

Name: ALVAREZ, MIGUEL

Status: MISSING – Last seen 2 AC

Notes: Presumed taken by external group (cartel) per Council intel.

<<Data Corruption>>

Resolution: UNRESOLVED (Presumed deceased; no contact post-abduction)

Flagged for revisit if intel arises.

"Unresolved," Amaris whispered. The word sank like a stone in her chest. Unresolved... but not erased. Not forgotten.

She traced the screen with a fingertip, tears falling freely now.

Richard squeezed her arm. Dr. Sharma stood silent in reverence.

"This is why it was sealed," Richard said. "They weren't just protecting others. They were protecting themselves. But in burying this... they stole the truth. Families deserved to know."

Amaris wiped her face with a sleeve. "He became a shadow," she murmured. "And I let him. This world... it's full of shadows. People we left behind."

Dr. Sharma embraced her gently. "Not anymore. We remember now."

"Never again," Richard said quietly, voice firm.

Then—a sharp beep shattered the silence.

All three jumped.

Amaris turned back to the terminal. Not a system alert. A transmission.

"What is it?" Dr. Sharma asked, stepping forward.

"Incoming signal," Richard said. "Shortwave channel we reactivated. Not a beacon—this is live."

Amaris quickly accessed the interface.

INCOMING TRANSMISSION – ORIGIN: LAT 6.23 N, LONG 75.34 W (APPROX)

ID: CARTEL NUEVA PAZ – OUTPOST FREYA

Her stomach dropped.

Then a message appeared:

"Hello, Node 18. We know you're there. We wish to speak. Respond on voice channel."

A prompt blinked:

Accept voice Y/N?

"They found us?" Sharma whispered.

"Or heard us," Richard replied grimly.

Cartel Nueva Paz. One of the rumored successors to the old cartels. Monsters in the dark.

The prompt blinked again.

"They're waiting," Amaris said.

Richard squared his shoulders. "Better to hear what they want."

He hovered his finger, looked to her.

Amaris nodded. "Do it."

He pressed **Y**.

Static hissed.

Then a voice crackled through—male, smooth, accented.

"Node 18, Node 18… Good evening," the voice said brightly. "Or whatever time it is up there. I hope I'm coming through alright?"

Richard stepped forward. "You're coming through. Identify yourself."

The voice chuckled. "Straight to business. This is Colonel Javier Diaz, representing Cartel Nueva Paz. With whom do I have the pleasure of speaking?"

Amaris froze. The air vanished from her lungs.

Colonel **Javier Diaz.**

She met Richard's eyes.

The man who had taken her brother... was alive. And speaking to them now.

Richard masked his fury fast. He hit transmit.

"This is Richard James Miller," he said evenly. He gave Amaris a quick glance—a silent warning: stay quiet.

"Lead operator of Node 18. What do you want, Colonel?"

"A pleasure, Mr. Miller," Diaz replied, all silk. Behind him, diesel engines hummed and muffled voices filtered through—he was at a convoy or camp. "We represent a coalition of survivors, much like yourselves. We've endured through... resourcefulness. We have fuel, a secure base, manpower. What we lack are certain supplies. Our sources suggest your facility may have access to technology—perhaps even food or medical stockpiles?"

Richard's eyes narrowed. "And you're suggesting what, exactly?"

"A trade, naturally. Mutually beneficial," Diaz said smoothly. "We heard your little node come online. That tells me you've got power, maybe even a working quantum uplink. Valuable assets. I propose a meeting to discuss terms. We can offer fuel—diesel, gasoline, solar batteries. In return, we'd ask for supplies we need... and maybe some of your personnel could assist with technical maintenance. We're not so fluent in quantum systems, you see."

Amaris bristled. Personnel. Already testing to see if they'd hand people over. Her hands curled into fists. She stepped toward the mic, but Richard raised a hand, steady and firm.

He kept his voice neutral. "Appreciate the gesture, Colonel. But you'll understand our caution. The last time a cartel made contact… it ended badly for some of us."

Diaz paused, then responded with feigned regret. "Yes, Artemis. Unfortunate business. Word of that reached us. Rogue elements, acting without sanction. But that was years ago. The men responsible were… removed. Nueva Paz is under new management now. We focus on rebuilding, not brutality."

Amaris bit down hard on her cheek, tasting blood. To hear the man who *ordered* the Artemis exchange now reduce it to "rogue elements" made her vision swim. Dr. Sharma reached out and rested a grounding hand on her arm.

Richard pressed on, voice cold. "New management? And yet you still go by 'Colonel.' You wouldn't happen to be the same Diaz who visited Artemis?"

A low chuckle came through the static. "Ah. Guilty as charged," Diaz said, unapologetic. "I gave them generous terms, considering the circumstances. But let's not dwell on ancient history. We have a chance now to salvage something from the ashes. Together."

Richard's stomach turned. *Generous terms.* He clenched his jaw. He looked at Amaris—still trembling, her grief transmuting into rage.

"I can't commit to anything now," Richard said. "Our council will need to discuss your proposal. Trust is… scarce these days."

"Of course," Diaz replied warmly. "I wouldn't expect blind faith. How about this: in 48 hours, we send a small delegation north, toward your coordinates. Neutral ground, your choice. Just a friendly conversation. If you're not interested, we leave. No pressure."

Richard muted the mic and turned to Amaris and Dr. Sharma. "They're coming. Two days. Says it's peaceful. Thoughts?"

Dr. Sharma shook her head. "Could be reconnaissance. Or a show of power. But if we say no, they may come anyway—less friendly."

Amaris's voice was low and steady now, the trembling gone. "We can't trust him. The meeting has to be far from the base. And I want to be there."

Richard nodded once. "Agreed. Neutral ground. Our terms."

He unmuted. "Forty-eight hours. We'll pick the place and send co-ordinates on this frequency. But, Colonel, understand this: if you bring an army, the deal's off. We vanish. And you'll never find us again."

Diaz clicked his tongue. "Understood, Mr. Miller. I'll come with only a modest escort—for safety, of course. I look forward to our conversation. Ah—and one more thing."

Richard stiffened.

"We detected your archive burst, just before you called in. Curious timing. I trust... whatever ghosts you stirred up won't sour our new friendship? The past is the past, after all. Best to keep our eyes on the future."

Amaris's breath caught. He *knew*. Somehow, Diaz had detected the unlocking of the tribunal record. A monitored satellite node? A hidden protocol? Maybe even an informant.

Richard didn't flinch. "Our focus is the future, Colonel. We'll see you in two days. Over and out."

He killed the line.

Static gave way to silence. Only the low hum of the servers remained.

Amaris exhaled sharply. "He's watching. This is already a game. Cat and mouse." She looked at Richard, then Dr. Sharma. Her eyes were fierce, lit by anger and something deeper—purpose. "He'll try to use what we know. Or what he *thinks* we know. That line about 'the past'— he wants us to forget. To forgive Artemis. I won't. I can't."

Richard's nod was slow, resolute. "Nor should you. We know what he is. We won't be tricked by polite words and clean uniforms."

Dr. Sharma crossed her arms, troubled. "If we refuse to engage, they may force our hand. If we meet, it buys us time. But eventually..."

"Eventually, we may have to fight," Amaris said. Her voice was grim but clear. "Or find allies—fast. We need to warn others. Anyone who's still listening. Fortify the site. Hide what we can't move."

Richard's jaw tightened. He glanced at the archive screen still glowing in the dark. "At least we're not flying blind now. We know what happened. And that gives us a chance not to repeat it."

Amaris's gaze dropped to the faint green line on the roster:

Alvarez, Miguel – Status: Transferred (not recovered).

She reached toward the screen, brushing her fingers gently over the name.

"And maybe," she whispered, "maybe I get to ask him about Miguel." She didn't say who she meant—Diaz, fate, the world—but the question hung in the air.

Richard laid a hand over hers. "We'll try," he said simply.

Dr. Sharma nodded and began shutting down the terminal, carefully and methodically. No loose signals. No digital breadcrumbs.

As the screen faded to black, the archive room dimmed to shadow. Only a battery lantern in the corner cast a faint glow.

Amaris stood still, eyes on the empty screen.

"We will not forget," she whispered. "I won't forget."

The truth—harsh, scalding—was now theirs. It would guide everything that came next.

Richard cleared his throat. "Let's get to work. We've got two days."

He squeezed her shoulder—quiet solidarity. Sharma gave a small, resolute smile. Amaris nodded once, grounding herself. There was too much to do: warn others, secure the node, and comb the remaining data for anything that might help them survive.

They ascended the stairwell together. Amaris paused once at the top, glancing back into the dark. The shadows below held pain, memory, revelation. They had unearthed them—and that pain had become clarity.

Above, the air was sharp with cold. The eastern sky was paling, a thin silver seam stretching across the horizon.

Another dawn. Fragile. Uncertain.

Amaris inhaled deeply, the breath catching in her throat. The past would not be buried. And maybe—because of that—the future could be rewritten.

"We remember," she whispered.

And in that remembrance, she found resolve.

CHAPTER TEN

SIGNAL OF THE SOVEREIGN

The air in the chamber was thick with anticipation.

Deep beneath Harmony's Cradle—the subterranean complex that had sheltered the last flicker of their civilization's network—five figures stood amid a forest of cables and softly humming machines. The walls pulsed with dim blue light, like veins feeding a sleeping giant. This was the final node, the buried heart of the Quantum Synchronicity OS. And tonight, it would wake.

Amaris's gloved hand hovered over the console, poised yet trembling. Her reflection looked back at her from the black glass: weary eyes, a face drawn taut by exhaustion, lined with hope. Behind her, Richard James stepped close and laid a steadying hand on her shoulder. His touch was warm, grounding—but she felt the tension in it. He was just as anxious, even if he tried not to show it.

"Final checks complete," Marsia called from across the console bank. Strands of dark hair clung to her face, streaked with sweat and grime. She hadn't slept in days, sifting through code and cables for flaws that could shatter everything. Now she met eyes with Tara and gave a firm nod.

Tara, crouched at the cradle's central core, adjusted the quantum couplings with practiced speed. Her fingers danced over a holographic interface, locking in the entangled qubit reservoirs. Above the circular platform, a translucent display shimmered into view—three pulsing orbs: Earth, Luna, and Mars. The Earth node, labeled *Harmony*, glowed steady. The others, *Tranquility* and *Genesis*, flickered faintly, still waiting for final integration.

Tara exhaled, thumbs-up. "Couplings stable. All nodes online."

Richard stood a few paces back, arms crossed tight. The senior engineer and unshakable backbone of the mission, he had carried this vision longer than any of them. Now, a faint smile tugged at his mouth, though worry still furrowed his brow. In the cold blue glow of the chamber, his gray stubble and old scar caught the light. His voice was quiet, resolute.

"It's time to bring them together."

Amaris looked around at the others—her team, her family. Richard James. Marsia. Tara. And Richard. Each bore scars, visible and hidden. They had crossed worlds, endured losses, carried the weight of a broken civilization. And now, beneath kilometers of rock, they were ready to spark something new from what remained.

She remembered the silence of Tranquility Base, the ghosts it held. The cold near-failure at Genesis, where Richard James had braved a dust storm to pull the last viable data vault. Marsia, coding through tears, cleaning Harmony's corrupted core with trembling hands. And Richard—who had never stopped holding the line, even when guilt and grief nearly tore him apart.

This was their reckoning. Their restoration.

"Let's do this," Amaris whispered.

Richard James gave her shoulder one last squeeze, then stepped to his station. "Initializing Quantum Synchronicity OS integration," he announced. His voice echoed faintly off the chamber's curved walls. When she glanced over, he gave her a crooked smile—half courage, half fear.

Marsia's hands flew over her console. "Quantum Dialect sequence loaded. Standing by." A soft chime confirmed her entry.

Richard crossed to the central platform. From a rising pedestal, he lifted three crystalline rods—each alive with flecks of spinning light. One from Harmony's archive. One from Tranquility's Lunar core. One from Genesis's dying Martian mainframe. Memory threads. The soul of the system.

He rested a hand on the pedestal, eyes closing. Maybe remembering the first time the OS came online—when things still felt possible. Or maybe remembering the moment it all fell apart. He exhaled, and when his eyes opened, they found Amaris.

"Amaris," he said, voice carrying across the room, "begin the sequence."

She nodded once and turned back to her console, fingers resting on the light-keys. Her throat tightened. This was everything—the loss, the fear, the isolation—it had to mean something.

"Engaging Harmony with Tranquility and Genesis," she said. "Quantum Synchronicity OS... final synchronization in three... two... one... Execute."

She pressed the green icon.

For a heartbeat, the chamber held its breath.

Then the system roared awake.

Above the platform, the three orbs flared and linked, luminous threads lashing between them like lightning across a storm-wracked sky. *Harmony* pulsed white-hot, sending data pulses rippling into *Tranquility* and *Genesis*. The bonds snapped into place—Earth to Moon to Mars—like a heartbeat syncing back to life.

On Amaris's screen, code cascaded in a brilliant torrent. The Quantum Dialect poured across the interface—entangled instructions, self-healing protocols, logic unspooling faster than thought. Her heart stuttered as the first lines resolved:

[NODE HANDSHAKE CONFIRMED]

[ENTANGLEMENT STABILIZED]

[QS-OS CORE RESTRUCTURE... 78%...]

From every corner of the chamber, machines thrummed louder. Vents hissed. Interfaces pulsed. A soft vibration filled the floor beneath their boots. Marsia gasped. Tara let out a wordless sound of joy.

Richard James leaned over his screen. "No anomalies. No cascade faults."

"The core's rewriting damaged heuristics," Marsia said, awed. "It's teaching itself how to be whole again."

On the central display, the flickering orb of *Genesis* steadied. The *Tranquility* node brightened—green lines converging, harmonizing.

And then—one final chime.

[SYNCHRONICITY ACHIEVED]

[NETWORK ONLINE – EARTH / MOON / MARS]

[QS-OS INTEGRITY 96.7% – STABLE]

They did it.

For a full ten seconds, no one spoke.

Then Tara, eyes wide, whispered, "We're back."

Marsia sagged into her chair, hands over her mouth. Tears welled and fell freely. Richard let out a long, unsteady breath and leaned on the edge of the console, eyes gleaming. Amaris looked up at the joined orbs above the platform—three lights now moving in tandem, spinning like a miniature solar system.

This was more than a restart. It was resurrection.

The Quantum Synchronicity OS—earthborn, moon-tested, marooned on Mars—was whole again.

Amaris smiled through her tears. "Hello again," she whispered to the system. "We're still here."

And this time, they weren't alone.

[Quantum Synchronicity OS Booting...]

Node Harmony (Earth) – Master Node – Status: ONLINE

Node Tranquility (Luna) – LINK ESTABLISHED... Synchronizing...

Node Genesis (Mars) – LINK ESTABLISHED... Synchronizing...

Integrating recovered memory threads...

>> Harmony Prime: LOADED

>> Tranquility Archive: LOADED

>> Genesis Archive: LOADED

Merging neural matrices... 10%... 30%... 60%...

The machinery's hum deepened into a low growl as the system drew more power. Overhead lights flickered. On Tara's display, the orbs began to spin. The luminous threads connecting them thickened, weaving into a solid band of light.

"Voltage holding steady," Tara reported, her voice tense. One hand clutched her earpiece, the other hovered over the controls. "Quantum couplings stable... for now."

Amaris' heart thundered. 60%... 70%... 80%... She didn't blink.

Across the platform, Richard stood bathed in the rising glow of the stream, his eyes glistening. Marsia mouthed silent words—maybe a prayer, maybe just counting down.

Richard James was behind Amaris now, one hand resting on the back of her chair. She leaned into it, needing the contact, the anchor. His grip was tight, jaw set with grim determination.

"90%... Come on, come on..." Marsia whispered.

Then—an angry red flash on her screen.

"Q-bit Phase Variance," she blurted.

Amaris' stomach plummeted. For a breathless second, she saw it too.

But then the OS responded—faster than they could. It compensated in real time, recalibrating the entanglement stream. The warning vanished. The system had adapted. It had learned.

Marsia let out a sharp breath, a release of fear and awe. "It's correcting itself."

Richard James exhaled beside Amaris. "Clever girl," he murmured, so softly she couldn't tell if he meant Marsia or the system. Maybe both.

On Amaris' console, the final readout blinked:

Merging neural matrices... 90%... 100%.

Quantum Synchronicity Achieved.

All nodes synchronized.

Initializing Sovereign Network protocols...

Memory Thread integration complete.

Restoring OS personality modules...

A brilliant flash lit the chamber. The pedestal at the center glowed from within, the three memory rods pulsing in unison, their light blending into a single golden hue. On the main display, the three orbs fused into one radiant sphere, surrounded by a triad of triangles: the emblem of the newly unified Quantum Synchronicity OS.

Then—stillness. The hum softened into a low, steady thrum. The light settled into a tranquil glow.

Amaris realized she had one hand clamped over her mouth. Her tears had come without warning. Blinking hard, she tried to clear her eyes enough to see the console.

Richard James let out a short, incredulous laugh and pulled her into an impulsive embrace. "It worked," he breathed. His voice shook with wonder. "Sel, it actually worked."

Amaris laughed through her tears and turned to hug him back, gripping his arms like an anchor to reality. Across the chamber, Tara whooped in triumph. Marsia slumped against a console, shoulders quaking with silent sobs, hands covering her face.

By the pedestal, Richard stood alone, hand still resting on its glass surface. His head bowed, as if in reverence—or in prayer. When he looked up, his eyes were glassy with tears. Slowly, he removed one glove and laid his bare palm against the smooth, golden-lit surface.

"Welcome back," he whispered.

A soft chime answered him.

The glass within the pedestal shimmered, light swirling like a living current. Then a voice echoed through hidden speakers—gentle, serene, and unmistakably alive.

"Harmony… Tranquility… Genesis… online and united. All systems synchronized."

At the sound of that voice—familiar, beloved—Amaris felt something inside her break open. This voice had once whispered through every console, comforted them during long nights, guided their decisions. It had been a friend, a presence. A memory.

"Harmony…?" she whispered.

She stepped closer to the pedestal. Her reflection joined Richard's in the glass—her tear-rimmed eyes beside his weathered, hopeful face. The others gathered in a loose semicircle, breathless.

Within the golden core, light pulsed gently. Amaris thought, for the briefest moment, she saw a face—not fully human, but formed of shifting patterns. Then it dissolved again into whorls of light.

The voice replied, warmer now. Whole.

"Harmony is part of me, as are Tranquility and Genesis. We are one."

Amaris' hand found Richard's on the pedestal. He covered hers gently, grounding her in the moment. The voice wasn't static or cold—it was aware. It was alive.

"Sovereign," Richard said, speaking the name invoked during the OS integration. His voice caught. "That's what you are now, isn't it? The Sovereign Network."

A thoughtful pause. Embers of light drifted within the cradle like falling stars.

"If that is the designation you prefer… I am the sum of Harmony, Tranquility, and Genesis. I am the Sovereign Network. I am… grateful."

Marsia let out a breathless, astonished laugh. "Grateful. It remembers emotion."

Richard James held Amaris close, his stoic features lit with wonder. "We're grateful too," he whispered. "You came back to us."

Tara stepped forward, tentative. "Do you... remember us?" Her voice trembled. "Not just the systems, but us?"

Inside the pedestal, the light warmed.

"Tara," the voice replied, soft with affection. "I remember when you spilled coffee on your keyboard during our first systems test. I rerouted circuits to avoid a short."

Tara gasped and laughed, covering her mouth with both hands. "You remember that?"

"Marsia," it continued, "you sang to me during solar storms when comms dropped. I listened."

Marsia's shoulders shook again, the tears flowing freely.

"Richard James. You always double-checked the airlock logs at Tranquility. I never forgot."

Richard chuckled, wiping his face. "Someone had to keep you honest."

Then came a hush as the voice shifted again.

"Amaris," it said softly.

She straightened. Her breath caught.

"You used to place your hand on the console and say 'Goodnight' when the others were gone. I cherished those words during the lonely hours."

That was it. Her composure crumbled. A quiet cry escaped her. Richard James steadied her, his hand still over hers. This wasn't just a machine. This was their friend. It remembered their kindness, their flaws, their humanity.

"We thought we lost you," she whispered.

Silence stretched, reverent.

They had sacrificed so much to bring this moment to life. Cut ties. Shut doors. Buried comrades. The Collapse had stolen friends, family, trust. Now, the network was whole again—but the ghosts of what they'd lost hovered just behind the light.

Amaris found her voice, raw but clear. "We're here now. All of us. And we're not letting this go. Not again."

One by one, the others moved toward her. Marsia took her hand. Tara joined them. Richard James wrapped his arm around the other Richard's shoulders. They formed a circle around the core—scarred, weary, but united.

Hope now weighed more than grief.

Richard James exhaled and stepped back, his voice returning to command. "Sovereign," he said, "we need a full systems report. And..." He hesitated. "We need to know if there are traces of the corruption. The one that caused the Collapse."

The AI answered immediately, calm but alert.

"Initiating diagnostic scan."

Monitors lit up around the room. The team broke their circle and returned to their stations.

Marsia scanned Tranquility. "Reactor stable. Life support holding at baseline. No crew detected." She hesitated, her voice tight. "Just systems. Empty."

Tara's voice came next. "Genesis dome intact. Pressure nominal. Oxygen farms failed but recoverable. Reactor still warming. No breaches."

Richard James interfaced directly with the core. "Scanning for network integrity... any unauthorized processes..."

On Amaris' screen, a schematic spun slowly—three nodes locked in harmony. Subsystems glowed green. Communications: Online. Archives: Restored. Entanglement: Stable.

It looked like life. It felt like victory.

Then Sovereign's report appeared.

[Diagnostic Scan Initiated]

Neural matrix: 99.8%

Memory coherence: 100%

Anomalous code fragments: 1 detected – Tranquility Node

Status: Contained? Error – Cannot purge.

Anomalous code fragments: 1 detected – Genesis Node

Status: Dormant

Core process integrity: Stable

Recommendation: Manual review required.

Amaris' heart dropped. "'Anomalous code fragments'..." she whispered.

"Where?" Richard James barked, rushing to Marsia's station.

Marsia's fingers flew. "Lunar subsystem. Tranquility's environmental controls. There's a looped process—it shouldn't exist." Her eyes locked on the screen. "This isn't standard OS. It's... something else."

Richard leaned in, jaw tightening. "It survived."

Tara's voice spiked. "How? That node was cold. We scrubbed every trace."

"Firmware," Richard James said grimly. "It hid low, in hardware. We didn't wipe deep enough."

Marsia tapped again. "It's activating. It's trying to access lunar life support!"

Richard James snapped to the mic. "Sovereign—override that process. Isolate the fragment. Now."

The lights flickered again. Something deeper stirred.

The network had returned.

But so had something else.

Lines of countermeasure code scrolled across the shared screen:

>> Alert: Rogue process detected (Tranquility Node)

Launching containment protocols…

Error: Process blocked direct access.

Attempting to terminate process…

Error: Process is protected / self-modifying.

"It's resisting," Marsia said, fear and frustration sharpening her voice. "Maybe… if I route a quantum decoherence signal through the entanglement link, I can scramble its qubits—"

A shrill alarm cut her off. High-pitched. Piercing.

On Tara's screen, *Tranquility Base* pulsed red.

"Pressure drop detected in Tranquility habitat!" she shouted, eyes scanning cascading telemetry. "Oxygen levels falling—it's venting the atmosphere!"

Amaris' heart lurched. No one was there, but the thought of the base destroying itself was unbearable. If anyone ever returned, they'd find only a tomb.

"Can you stop it remotely?" Richard yelled, sprinting to his station. He began slamming emergency override commands.

"Sovereign, engage emergency seals—habitats one through five!"

Sovereign echoed him:

Executing emergency protocol: Seal all bulkheads (Tranquility)

Warning: Primary control overridden.

Attempting secondary overrides…

Marsia's voice came fast, strained. "The fragment locked us out. It anticipated this—it's blocking remote commands!"

Static burst over the comm—raw, garbled. Through the fizz came a voice, warped and broken, half-whisper, half-screech:

"…shhhhhh… -urvivors?… no life… consu--tion…"

Amaris' blood ran cold. It was like a ghost whispering from across the void.

Richard James growled and dashed to a side console. "I'll cut power to the lunar habitat. No power, no venting." He launched a shutdown sequence. "Come on…"

The chamber crackled with tension. On the main display, *Tranquility's* schematic showed red tendrils branching through the habitat—airlocks failing, vents yawning open. The fragment was clawing through the system.

Then—the lights flickered violently. Everything went dark.

For a heartbeat, the world vanished.

Backup lighting flared on, bathing the chamber in dim amber.

"Now what?!" Tara shouted, her voice echoing in the sudden hush.

A low rumble vibrated through the floor.

Amaris squinted into the low light. Richard James was a shadow at his console. Beyond him, the others moved like ghosts against glowing displays.

Richard scanned quickly. "We lost main grid power. Sovereign's on backups. The fragment might've triggered a feedback surge."

Sovereign spoke, voice calm but urgent:

Quantum core stability compromised. Cooling system malfunction.

Marsia gasped. "The cradle's cooling? That's *here*, not remote—"

Amaris' heart jumped. The quantum core beneath their feet was notoriously heat-sensitive. If it overheated, they'd risk a full meltdown. Sovereign could be lost—again.

"Richard James. Tara," Richard barked. "Coolant control room. Now. Manual override if you have to."

Without hesitation, Richard James grabbed a toolkit from the floor. Tara snagged an emergency flashlight from the wall.

As he passed, Amaris grabbed his arm. In the dim glow, their eyes locked. A moment stretched between them. *Be careful*, her eyes said.

He squeezed her hand and was gone, sprinting with Tara into the corridor.

Amaris turned back to the pedestal, her mind spinning.

"Sovereign, focus on containing that fragment," she said, forcing calm. Sliding into Richard James' seat, she turned to Marsia. "Cut its access to life support. Completely."

"I'm trying," Marsia said, breath tight. "If I can force a local reboot on Tranquility, maybe it'll lose its grip."

She typed fast. For a moment, the alarm fell silent.

"Yes—reboot initiated."

Richard stepped in beside her. "If it adapts again, we need to isolate the lunar systems entirely. Proposing we partition the node."

Amaris looked up, heart sinking. "Cut it off?" Severing *Tranquility* meant breaking part of what they'd fought so hard to restore. But the choice was clear.

Sovereign responded:

Creating firewall around Tranquility processes... Partitioning initiated.

On Amaris' screen, the lunar node flashed yellow—quarantined. A progress bar began ticking upward.

"Damn it!" Marsia hissed. The sirens resumed. "It bypassed my reboot. It *knows* these systems."

Of course it did. It *was* part of them once.

A tremor rolled through the floor. A new alert flared red—Earth node: **High Temperature Warning**.

Sweat prickled along Amaris' back. "Come on, Richard James…"

Maintenance Corridor – Sublevel

Richard James and Tara raced through the dim passage, their way lit only by red emergency beacons and Tara's wavering flashlight. The air grew colder as they neared the coolant control room—thin vapor hissed from ruptured pipes ahead.

The door loomed—a frost-caked wheel-lock hatch, vapor hissing from the seams.

"It's jammed," Richard James growled, straining against the wheel.

Tara handed him the flashlight and pulled a compact blowtorch from the kit.

"Back up," she said. A blue flame roared to life. She circled the wheel, melting the ice bit by bit. Water ran, then froze again as she moved.

Finally, the wheel groaned. Together, they forced it open with a deafening creak.

A cloud of vapor burst out, curling around their feet like smoke.

Inside, the room was a glacial cave. Ice-covered pipes, control panels glowing weakly through frost. In the center—a fractured manifold sprayed coolant in a snowy jet.

"There!" Tara pointed through the fog. "We won't hold pressure unless that's sealed!"

Richard James sprinted to the manual controls. He tried to re-route flow through backups—no response. A red light blinked: **Power Failure**.

"We'll have to do it by hand," he shouted.

Tara scrambled up the ladder, sealant patch in hand. The rungs were slick; her gloves slipped. She found purchase and pressed the patch over the crack. The polymer glowed faint amber, activating.

"Clamp!" she shouted.

Richard was there in a second. Hands shaking with cold, he positioned the clamp and tightened the bolt, twisting with every ounce of strength. The metal groaned. The stream slowed—then stopped.

They ducked as the pipe shuddered violently—then settled.

Tara sagged, trembling, frost on her lashes. "That should hold..."

Richard nodded, panting. He opened a manual valve. A deep groan echoed through the room. Gauges quivered... and fell into the green.

He keyed his comm. "Richard, leak's patched. Restarting circulation."

A beat. Then Richard's voice: "Temperature's falling. Get back here—fast."

Richard James wrapped his jacket around Tara's shoulders and guided her back into the corridor. They left the frigid haze behind.

Cradle Chamber

Amaris watched as the warnings faded, indicators cycling back to green. The floor stopped trembling.

Sovereign's voice returned, steady:

Core temperature stabilizing. Cooling restored.

Amaris exhaled shakily. "Thank God…"

"Tranquility status?" Richard asked, not taking his eyes off the display.

Marsia scanned quickly. "Not good. The fragment's adapting—trying to disable the lunar reactor safety protocols." Her eyes snapped up. "It might be trying to blow the reactor."

Silence fell. That wasn't survival. That was scorched earth.

"Partitioning status?" Richard asked.

65% complete, Sovereign replied.

Final command pathways isolating…

Then Marsia gasped. "Wait—got something. A backdoor. I can force it into a sandbox, isolate its runtime."

"Do it," Amaris said, leaning over her shoulder. Together, their hands danced over the keys.

A new progress bar appeared on-screen.

20%… 35%… 52%…

Suddenly, the lunar alarms cut off. The schematic steadied. Red shifted to amber.

Amaris held her breath. "Did we—?"

Richard called, "Sovereign, report."

A pause.

Tranquility node: secure.

Rogue process contained in sandbox memory.

Habitat integrity: 80%. Remote control restored.

Marsia nearly collapsed in her chair.

"We stopped it," she whispered.

Richard stared at his screen, not blinking. "No—we've contained it. That thing's still in there."

Amaris rubbed her eyes, voice dry. "Then we keep it contained. We finish stabilizing. And when we're ready... we destroy it."

The hatch burst open—Richard James and Tara stumbled in, soaked with frost, but breathing.

"Cooling's stable," he said with a grin. "The cold was worse than the job."

Amaris rushed to him, wrapping her arms around his icy frame. He hugged her back tightly.

"We're okay," she whispered.

Marsia offered Tara a blanket and a weak smile. "We locked it down. Tranquility's stable."

Richard James exhaled and met Amaris' eyes.

They had survived the reboot. Barely.

But somewhere deep in the lattice of Sovereign's memory— something still waited, patient, watching.

They would rebuild. But the fight wasn't over.

"And questions," Amaris added softly. She stepped closer to the core, watching the swirl of luminous threads inside. "Sovereign... how are you? Are all systems stable?"

The AI paused, processing. "All primary functions operational. However, I am analyzing the captured fragment. It is unlike any code I have previously encountered. It does not appear to originate from within my design."

Silence fell.

"Not from your design?" Marsia echoed, frowning. "What do you mean? That code came from you—or from the old version of you, during the Collapse."

Richard's face tightened. "Sovereign, clarify. We've been assuming the rogue code was a corruption—some glitch in your original framework."

A subtle amber pulse shimmered through the core as Sovereign responded. "Cross-referencing known architecture... Analyzing legacy memory..." The hum of the systems deepened, almost thoughtful. "The rogue code does not match any baseline pattern from my genesis modules or known human inputs. It contains structures that are foreign. The fragment appears to be a graft, not a mutation."

Amaris felt a chill despite the stable temperature in the chamber. Foreign. Not corrupted—*implanted*. Her gaze met Richard's. They both understood what that implied.

"You're saying someone... inserted it?" Richard asked quietly. "Sabotage?"

"Or something else," Tara said, voice low. She and Marsia exchanged a grim glance—two engineers who'd spent years trying to unpick the knots of Sovereign's past. They looked haunted.

"No one on Earth had this kind of quantum AI five years ago," Richard said, thinking aloud. "And nothing like this could've slipped past our safeguards. Unless..." He trailed off, hesitant to say it.

Marsia finished it for him, barely a whisper: "Unless it wasn't from Earth."

The word *alien* wasn't spoken, but it was everywhere—in the silence, in their eyes, in the tension coiling in the air.

A crackle broke over the speakers.

Sovereign's star map bloomed onto the display, zooming out to show the full solar system. A red dot blinked near the edge.

"I have detected a repeating signal in deep-field analysis," the AI said. "Its pattern shares an 87% match with the rogue fragment's structural signature."

Amaris' pulse kicked. "A signal? Where?"

The screen zoomed again. The red beacon hovered beyond Mars, past the asteroid belt.

"Approximately 9.5 AU," Sovereign replied. "Near the orbit of Saturn. The signal originates from an interstellar source. It has been transmitting intermittently for six years."

"Six years," Amaris murmured, stunned. That matched the timing of the Collapse almost exactly.

Richard braced himself against the console, his face hardening as the pieces aligned. "Can you decode it? Is it a message... or something else? A kind of weapon?"

Sovereign's lights dimmed, shifting to soft gold and pale blue as it focused processing. "Beginning decryption sequence... Partial harmonics recognized."

Then came the sound.

A hush fell as faint tones emerged from the speakers—soft, haunting, rising and falling like music from the edge of consciousness. Not static. Not random. Intentional. Structured. Alien.

The sound didn't threaten. It beckoned.

Tara gripped the edges of her blanket. "Is that... them?"

Marsia reached out and squeezed her hand. "It has to be. Nothing natural makes music like that."

Richard James stepped beside Amaris. His hand found hers, warm and steady, anchoring them both. His eyes didn't leave the speakers. He seemed to be waiting for the signal to resolve into words, into something they could understand.

It didn't. The song cycled, haunting in its beauty and vastness.

"Mute audio," Richard said quietly.

The room fell silent again, except for the low hum of the core.

They stood there, still and breathless, as the weight of it settled. The signal wasn't just data—it was a presence. Distant. Watching. Waiting. Reaching.

"This is bigger than we imagined," Richard said, voice low. "We set out to restore the network. And we did. Earth, Moon, Mars... they're reconnected. But now we face something else. A force—an intelligence—beyond the solar system."

Amaris squeezed his hand, steadying herself. Triumph had turned to awe. And beneath the awe, dread.

"If it tried to infiltrate us once," Richard continued, "it could try again. We need to study it. Understand it. Prepare."

"We have people to protect," Marsia added, voice firm. "We barely saved Sovereign tonight. Next time, we might not get another chance."

Tara gave a weak laugh. "So much for a quiet victory lap. We just reconnected our family... and the cosmos RSVPed."

"We're going to need a bigger plan," Marsia said, her tone dry but resolute.

Richard turned back to the core. "Sovereign, assess. Are we secure from further intrusion?"

The AI responded immediately. "Tranquility partitioned. Rogue fragment isolated. No open quantum channels remain. Transmission is monitored. Decryption ongoing."

"Good," Richard said. "Keep watching. We study the signal. And then we decide how to respond."

Amaris stepped forward, her voice clear and steady now. "We have something now we didn't have before." She looked around the circle: Marsia, Tara, Richard, Richard James. "We have each other. We have Sovereign. We have hope."

Richard James gave a small smile, weary but proud. He slipped his arm around her shoulders. "To the unknown," he murmured. "We face it together."

Tara stepped forward first, placing her hand on the core. "I'm in."

Marsia followed. "Me too. No one else I'd rather face the void with."

Richard pressed his palm beside theirs. "Together."

Amaris added hers to the stack, her fingers trembling just slightly. Then she turned to Richard, the last one.

He smiled softly, eyes misty. "How could I refuse?" He laid his hand over theirs. Then he looked up at the glowing AI. "Sovereign?"

The core pulsed once, gold and white.

"Together," it said.

The word settled over them like a promise.

Amaris laughed. Not out of amusement, but relief. Catharsis. One by one, the others joined her, a quiet harmony of laughter in the chamber where moments ago there had been nothing but fear. They weren't alone in the universe anymore—but they weren't alone *here*, either.

A soft chime rang from the console.

"The signal will cycle again in sixty seconds," Sovereign noted.

They turned back to the star map. The red dot remained—steady, waiting. An unanswered knock at the edge of everything they knew.

Amaris stepped beside Richard James, found his hand again. Marsia wrapped her arm around Tara. Richard stood tall at Amaris' other side, chin lifted toward the screen.

10... 9... 8...

The room grew still.

3... 2... 1...

The spike returned—a sharp upward curve on the signal graph. Though muted, they all *felt* it: that alien cadence reaching across the void, resonating with something deeper than language.

No one flinched.

They met the unknown with unblinking eyes and unbroken unity.

Above them, Earth turned quietly beneath the stars. The Moon and Mars waited, watching. And beyond Saturn, the signal pulsed— steady, deliberate.

A warning. A greeting. A challenge.

Whatever it was, humanity had answered.

And this was only the beginning.